Farm to Fabre

DAHLIA DONOVAN

HOT TREE PUBLISHING

Farm to Fabre

Dahlia Donovan

Hot Tree Publishing

Also by Dahlia Donovan

THE GRASMERE COTTAGE MYSTERY TRILOGY

DEAD IN THE GARDEN | DEAD IN THE POND | DEAD IN THE SHOP

MOTTS COLD CASE MYSTERY SERIES

POISONED PRIMROSE | PIERCED PEONY | PICKLED PETUNIA | PURLOINED POINSETTIA

LONDON PODCAST MYSTERY SERIES

COSPLAY KILLER | GHOST LIGHT KILLER | CROWN COURT KILLER

STAND-ALONE ROMANCES

AFTER THE SCRUM | AT WAR WITH A BROKEN HEART | FORGED IN FLOOD | FOUND YOU | BY THE FIRE | ONE LAST HEIST | PURE DUMB LUCK | HERE COMES THE SON | ALL LATHERED UP | NOT EVEN A MOUSE | FARM TO FABRE | THE MISGUIDED CONFESSION

THE SIN BIN (COMPLETE SERIES)

THE WANDERER | THE CARETAKER | THE ROYAL MARINE | THE BOTANIST | THE UNEXPECTED SANTA | THE LION TAMER | HAKA EVER AFTER | COMPLETE BOX SET

For information, contact the publisher, Hot Tree Publishing.

WWW.HOTTREEPUBLISHING.COM

EDITING: Hot Tree Editing

COVER DESIGNER: BooksSmith Design

E-book ISBN: 978-1-922679-43-7

PAPERBACK ISBN: 978-1-922679-44-4

*For anyone who has struggled to find the right words
to express how they feel or their sexuality.*

Chapter 1
Andie

January

IT IS TIME TO WAKE UP.

Feel yourself slowly floating to consciousness.

It is time to wake up.

"No." Andie slapped her hand absently against the nightstand, knocking over her bottle of water while hunting for her phone. She jabbed at it before holding it above her face and then frowned. "What do you mean, you don't recognise my face? It's my face. The faceiest of faces. It's the only one I have."

Dropping back onto the pillow, Andie scowled in the darkness. Her nonna had forced her to download the calming wake-up app. Unfortunately, it mostly made her feel like she'd joined a cult.

"Fine." Andie stretched her arm out to flip on a light. "Oh, that's unnecessarily bright. There. Now can you recognise my face? Thank you."

She managed to get the app turned off. How was it supposed to help her wake up in a good mood? All it had done was make her want to smash her phone with a hammer.

"Hello, Rups." Andie rolled over to scratch her farm dog, a four-year-old Airedale Terrier. She'd named him Rupert because he reminded her of a scruffy, grumpy old man.

"Are we ready for the morning? No, neither am I."

Andriana Milne-Marchetti ran the M & M Farm outside a little village in Aberdeenshire in Scotland. She'd taken over when her parents decided to retire and move to Sicily to spend time with her nonna and nonno. Her mother had wanted to be with her parents, as they were both getting older.

Andie's father came from old Scottish farming stock, and the farm had been in the Milne family for ages. They no longer had cows and sheep. Her parents had turned it into a fruit orchard when Andie was a little girl.

She adored the farm. It had been her childhood dream to have the run of the place. She had so many ideas, including running a pop-up supper for her friends in the village.

Farm to table, as it were.

Yes, it was lonely on the farm with just Rupert, but she loved it nonetheless.

"All right, you furry fiend, why don't we see what we can scrounge up for breakfast?" Andie checked the date on her phone and cursed. "Is it already the fourteenth? Doc's going to be here today."

Docherty Fabre was a family friend. He'd lived in the village for a while before deciding to travel. Something had happened to him, though.

Her father had called her a few weeks back, asking if she minded if Doc stayed at the farm. They had a small shed that had been converted into a living space. Nothing fancy. Just a bedroom and a bathroom. Andie had immediately invited him to stay for as long as he needed.

And I'm going to regret it when I can't handle my embarrassing crush.

Nope. Don't think about it. Hopefully, the more you ignore it, the easier it'll become to pretend nothing's there.

If I don't mention the awkward kiss under the apple trees, maybe he won't either.

Probably won't, since he ran off like a bloody coward.

Stumbling into the bathroom, Andie stared at her reflection in the mirror. She shoved her brown hair out of her dark brown eyes. It was almost time to give herself another trim. She'd begun cutting her own hair when her favourite hairdresser (and best friend) moved to Edinburgh.

She hadn't done the worst job. It was all one length, and she wore a beanie most days. So what did the slight unevenness to her pixie cut matter?

Rupert sat beside her, huffing at her when she reached for her moisturizer.

"I wasn't lucky enough to inherit Mama's smooth, tanned skin. I got Da's freckles and easily dried-out skin instead." Andie had learnt the hard way to liberally use moisturizer, particularly during the winter months. "I'll let you out in a moment. Hold your horses."

The farm cottage was an old stone home that her great-granddad had built. Her father had renovated some of it. But it retained the personality and creakiness of the original.

Old wooden floors that showed the passage of time and footsteps. Doorknobs that required opening a specific way to get them to cooperate. A smallish kitchen that had seen so many family memories.

Andie had considered completely redoing the interior of the cottage. She'd gone so far as to get quotes from contractors. But sitting at the old family kitchen table, one her great-grandfather had built, with her coffee and toast, she'd changed her mind.

The one thing Andie had done was install a new heating system. Electric radiators. She'd gotten one for the bedrooms and one in the kitchen. The living room had a working fireplace as well.

The cottage had felt so incredibly cramped with two bedrooms and one bathroom as a teenager. Now, on her own, it seemed almost cavernous. Especially on cold nights with no one but Rupert to keep her company.

Making her way through the kitchen, Andie opened the door for Rupert to rush out. She put the kettle on the stove and then raced back to the bedroom for her socks and a jumper. It was a crisp January morning.

Once Rupert returned from his morning ablutions, Andie set his breakfast down for him. She had a few slices of toast while cooking up some porridge. A hearty meal to stick with her through the long hours of working on the farm.

With breakfast done, Andie changed out of her pyjamas into what she jokingly called her farm girl uniform. Jeans, comfortable boots, a long-sleeved T-shirt plus a thick hoodie and a jacket in the winter. Layers. Layers mattered, since all the physical labour meant she'd want to shed a few items of clothing by midday.

Making her way outside with Rupert trotting ahead of her, Andie got to the easiest items on her to-do list. Or what she'd assumed to be the simplest. She hadn't expected to run into trouble when making sure all the plants were watered.

How wrong she was.

"Ah, you wee little bugger." Andie had been struggling with the irrigation system for her polytunnels all morning. She'd been trying to get it going for three hours. "Would you just bloody work?"

The answer was no.

It wouldn't.

Dragging an empty crate over, Andie sat down to contemplate her options. She didn't have time to run into the village for parts. She whistled for Rupert, who came bounding around the corner.

"What are you up to, Rups?" She scratched behind his ear while continuing to think. Maybe there was something in the tool shed to help get the water flowing. "We're going to have a visitor. I'll finally have someone to talk to that isn't furry."

Her dog gazed over at her.

"Not that there's anything wrong with talking to you. There isn't." Andie gave him one last good scratch, then pushed herself up off the crate. "They won't irrigate themselves, will they?"

The farm had rows and rows of polytunnels. It was how she managed to get her crops of berries planted in the winter ready for harvest. The strawberries arrived frozen, ready for her to take care of them.

The tunnels were composed of timber, arches made of galvanized steel tubing, and a super-thermal cover that had ventilation panelling on the sides and an irrigation system that ran overhead to cover the raised beds. The planting beds had been built with the help of another local farmer. They'd used reclaimed wood, which saved money.

But first, she had to get the irrigation system working.

Three hours.

Three actual hours.

Andie was covered in mud from head to toe by the time she finished. She'd wrestled the irrigation system into submission—found the damaged connection in the sixth polytunnel she'd checked. "Well, Rups? Think I've time for a shower before Doc arrives?"

"Odds are against you."

She smiled at the familiar low baritone behind her and then grimaced when she glanced down at her clothes. "You're early."

"I'm not. Your watch is obviously covered in whatever filth you've been rolling around in." He hadn't changed much since she'd seen him over Christmas a few years ago. Still a tall teddy bear of a man with a riot of wavy black hair now streaked with grey, as was his beard. "You've a wee bit of mud on you."

"Droll, Doc. Is that the word of the day? It should be. Droll." Andie stood up and stretched, trying to ignore the state of her clothes. She was relatively tall at just under six feet. He stood several inches taller. "What brings you to the wilds of Scotland? Mama didn't say."

"Writer's block." Doc grabbed his bag and stalked off in the direction of the little shed turned tiny home, throwing a worrying remark over his shoulder on the way. "I won't be a bother."

"You're never a bother. I would have spruced up the place if you were." Andie stared after him with a worrying combination of concern and confusion. Doc could occasionally be taciturn and often isolated himself; she'd always assumed it was part and parcel of his being autistic. But this seemed different, and she remembered her parents mentioning something had happened. "We're going to find out what's going on, Rups."

Somehow.

How hard could it be? She'd already fixed her irrigation system. It couldn't be as convoluted as that.

Could it?

"What do you think, Rupert? How complicated can the human head and heart be?" Andie chuckled when he dropped his head down. "You're probably right."

Chapter 2
Doc

January

FOR THE PAST THREE YEARS, DOC HAD BEEN travelling the world searching for inspiration. Mostly he'd found heartbreak and misunderstandings. And writer's block. He hadn't found words.

He'd lost them.

Somewhere in Venice or maybe Rome.

When his old friend Alex had offered a stay at the farm, Doc had gratefully accepted. He'd been ecstatic at a chance to be alone. Remove himself from people. From crowds. And then he'd considered who currently resided there.

Andie.

Andriana.

She'd been the reason for his flight from Scotland in the first place. They'd kissed. Once. Under an apple tree on Christmas Eve. It had surprised both of them.

There hadn't even been mistletoe involved.

And then he'd fled Scotland to avoid her.

Someone has to have written a song about kissing under an apple tree.

And about a fool in love who is also a cowardly lion.

He'd told himself it wasn't running away. Instead, he'd made a conscious decision to leave for both their sakes. She deserved better.

Better than a curmudgeon of an author who had fourteen or so years on her.

Then again, the age gap hadn't really bothered him that much. Her parents were twelve years apart in age. His mother had been ten years older than his father.

Maybe he'd just been too afraid to make the leap. Too afraid of feelings he struggled to understand, not wanting to delve too deeply into himself for fear of disappointing her.

"Knock, knock," Andie called, disrupting the swirling thoughts in his mind. "No. Rupert! Come back here."

It was his only warning before the Airedale came barging into the little house. He skittered around the small living area and then plopped down on his belly. His tail wagged when Doc reached down to give him a good scratch.

"He's not a bother." Doc waved off her concern when she inched her way into the tiny living room. "How can I help? I've barely unpacked."

"I know you have a word block to destroy, but I thought a warm meal by the fire might encourage the demolition?" Andie had always loved to cook, he remembered. It was almost like watching an artist create when she was in the kitchen, and almost as messy. "Nothing fancy, mind."

"Your idea of fancy cooking and mine are vastly different." Doc was a dab hand at only a few things in the kitchen. "You sure I won't be a bother?"

"Well, unless you've a fully stocked larder in your luggage, you're either going to starve or eat your meals with me." Andie eyed him up and down; her brown eyes always seemed to stare right into his soul. "I won't bite. I won't even kiss you, since the last time I did, you went running for the hills and over the seas."

"Andie." Doc winced at the direct blow she'd dealt him. "I'm—"

"I even baked my nonna's apple cake for you." Andie cut him off ruthlessly while picking at the threads of her clean cardigan. She'd changed out of her muddy clothes before coming to see him. "You'll come up for supper, right? In a couple of hours?"

"I will. How are your cats?" Doc blurted. He'd always found small talk uncomfortable, particularly with an underlying sense of guilt and unresolved tension in the air. "The barn cats."

Andie raised her eyebrows before breaking into a smile. "They're lovely. I've rescued a few more. I'll have to show you the home I've built for them. They're doing really well. Seem quite content to hang about, and Rups isn't bothering them. A win-win."

"I'll look forward to seeing them." Doc had thought about talking with Andie almost every day since he'd fled. He'd practised the speech he wanted to give her, yet all the words had vanished. His brain could occasionally be his worst enemy, so he settled for the mundane. "You've done wonders here with the farm."

"Doc." Andie dragged her fingers through her short hair, tugging at the ends. He thought she might be a little frustrated with him. Or maybe the situation. "I want us both to be comfortable here. We don't have to talk about what happened that Christmas."

"Don't we?"

"No."

Doc didn't think she necessarily believed it would be that easy either. "Can you pretend it never happened?"

"We've been doing a bloody good job of it up to this point. Why change now?" Andie reached out to pet Rupert when he whined up at her. "Sorry, Rups. I promise I'm not angry."

"Aren't you?"

Andie continued to peer down at Rupert. Doc had always appreciated how she never tried to force eye contact on him. "I'm not angry. I wasn't at the time either. Frustrated, if anything."

"Frustration feels like anger to me. But I'm sorry for leaving without speaking to you." Doc had figured Andie would be fine. He hadn't thought she'd be overly upset with his absence; he'd been wrong. "I'm sorry."

The silence grew between them. Doc enjoyed quiet most of the time, but he didn't like tension-filled moments when the calm was more of an anticipation of the coming storm.

Nodding jerkily at him, Andie backed out of the

room with Rupert close behind her. Doc sank into the nearest chair with a sigh. He scratched his jaw absently and briefly considered finding somewhere else to stay.

Running the first time hadn't solved anything. He had to deal with what happened. The consequences of his actions. He'd made the first move; maybe he shouldn't have.

Unrequited feelings weren't the worst thing in the world.

It's just a few months, and I'll be back travelling in no time at all. My heart will sort itself out.

Hopefully.

Chapter 3
Andie

January

"You're supposed to keep me calm, Rups." Andie had waited until they'd gotten out of view and hearing before collapsing against a nearby tree. She covered her face with her hands and tried not to scream into the wind. "I am so absolutely buggered. Oh. I am fucked. I thought I'd managed to put him out of my mind. Move on. He's still so... beautifully gruff."

Rupert, as always, offered her a supportive wag of his tail. It made her smile. A little. Andie pushed away from the tree. Her plants wouldn't water themselves.

Well, they would.

But that wasn't the point.

Fishing her headlight out of her pocket, Andie fixed it on her head. The sun had already gone down. It set so early in January. She used a strong LED lamp to see her way around in the darkness—handy for ensuring she didn't trip over tree limbs, rocks, or Rupert.

With the light blazing, Andie made a final walk through all of the polytunnels. The set-up allowed her to plant far earlier than she'd usually be able to. The raised beds and irrigation systems kept her seedlings flourishing through colder temperatures.

A quick check of her cats showed them all prowling about in the warmth of their cosy home. They did a fabulous job as chief mousers of her farm. She'd set up a lovely home and playground for them in one section of the barn.

"Shall we spy on the chickens, then head to the cottage?" Andie guided Rupert out of the structure. She shivered when the wind hit her; they were definitely in for a blustery evening. "Time to batten down the hatches."

It took a good hour to ensure nothing was going to fly away in the night. Finally, Andie made sure to turn the lights on around the cottage. She didn't want Doc to get lost in the dark; hopefully, he'd find the torch she'd left by the front door of the tiny house.

"Right. Shower first. Food after," Andie muttered to herself. She made sure Rupert had water and his meal before once again shedding her muddy clothes and dumping them in the laundry basket. "Here's hoping the entire evening isn't a complete disaster."

We can be friends.

We can just be friends.

It's okay that he's not interested in more. My heart can't break any more, can it? So I can be cool and calm.

And I am talking to myself.

The evening was already going to be fraught with tension. Andie opted for thick flannel pyjamas and a hoodie. Not flattering, but she wasn't fussed. Doc had already seen her completely covered in mud.

Cooking was usually a joy. Instead, today felt more like slow torment over hot coals. She'd narrowly avoided nicking her fingers while slicing up the mushrooms, kale, and sweet potato for her one-pot braised chicken dish.

It was hearty, warm, and filling. Also, it tended to

make enough for at least a few more meals. The dish went perfectly with the crusty bread she'd baked the day before.

She lit candles.

She never lit candles for supper unless the power went out or she wanted to be exceptionally cosy.

"Am I trying too hard?" Andie asked Rupert, who peered up at her before lying back down in the middle of the kitchen on a rug. "Could you put yourself any more in my way? You won't get any scraps if you make me fall on my knife."

I am trying too hard.

"Are the candles too much?" Andie didn't want Doc to feel pressured by the atmosphere. But she also wanted to be comfortable. "I'm overthinking this. Any suggestions, Rup?"

As per usual, Rupert was more excited by his treat than her blathering. Andie blew out the candles. They didn't need an "atmosphere" for supper on the farm.

Maybe I shouldn't be wearing flannel pyjamas.

Will he get the wrong idea?

Or maybe the right one?

She changed her outfit three times, managing to stop herself on the fourth since each one was almost identical to the last. T-shirt. Jeans. Cardigan. The only change had been the colours or design. *What am I even doing?* She returned to her pyjamas and hoodie.

Panicking. I am panicking. I should stop.

Pyjamas are fine.

By the time the stew was ready and Doc had arrived, Andie managed to calm herself. She could be calm. Normal. Not panicking. Friends had dinner all the time.

Doc hadn't spoken much when he arrived. He'd patted Rupert, then sat at the table with a muttered "Hello." He waited until she was ladling the braised chicken stew over the lentils to speak. "You seem anxious."

"What?" Andie dropped the spoon, spraying both of them with sauce. *Fuck.* "Oh for... I'm sorry."

"You seem anxious." Doc stared while she rushed to find a kitchen towel to clean the mess up. He reached out to grab her hands when she went to clean his shirt. "We're friends, right?"

"Right."

"So, calm down. We're both nervous over nothing at all. We'll eat. Talk about the weather or your berries or Rups." He released her hands, taking the towel from her and cleaning the sauce off his flannel shirt. "We're okay."

"Okay." Andie found herself getting lost in his eyes, enjoying their closeness for the briefest second, then stepping back. "Friends. And we're okay."

And I am so fucked.

Chapter 4
Doc

February

"I JUST WANT SOME BLOODY WORDS ON THE paper. Screen. Whatever. They don't have to be bloody. Regular ones would do." Doc glowered at his laptop. More specifically, he wished harm on the blank document and the flashing cursor mocking him. "How many times can I type and delete 'the' before it becomes an actual compulsion?"

Why am I talking out loud and asking myself rhetorical questions?

The blank page didn't respond, and the cursor continued to flash at him. Doc had been on the farm for a month already. He'd written maybe a thousand words in total—somehow managing to delete his progress the following day while editing.

Was it karmic retribution? He'd kissed and fled. Now all his words were running away on him.

There once was a man from....

Delete. Delete. Delete.

His agent and editor had both reached out to him, reminding him of his deadline. Not helpful. Words were already log-jammed in his mind, so focusing on a ticking clock wasn't conducive to resolving the problem.

Executive dysfunction had reared its ugly head as well. It made following a schedule or keeping his deadline in mind impossible, adding to the brain fog. At this rate, his book might never be finished.

Think positively.

Those were the words his agent threw at him. *Think positively.* He wasn't entirely sure how that might help. The page remained blank no matter how cheerfully he smiled at it.

"Doc? Can I come in?" Andie tapped on the window next to the front door. She waited until he waved her in to open the door. "I spoke with Mama."

"And how are the Italians faring this morning?" Doc closed his laptop, not even bothering to save the file. Why bother with a blank page? "Anything new in the spaghetti?"

"I'm going to ignore the bad joke." Andie grinned, but it seemed a little off to him. "The virus is picking up there faster than here."

Doc had been avoiding the news, for the most part. It tended to cause him immense stress about things he had zero control over. "Tell them to avoid crowds. Wear a mask."

"A mask?"

"I lived in Japan for a while. People wear masks to avoid spreading the flu. I can't imagine it hurting them to wear some sort of mask." Doc had appreciated the normalcy of it while he'd lived there. He wondered if he still had a few spare ones leftover from his last stay. "I'm sure they'll be fine."

"Aren't you worried?"

"We don't know enough for me to worry." Doc watched her pick at a loose button on her dungarees. "We'll take it all a day at a time. Not much else we can do."

"Want to walk some of the orchard and pasture by the road with me? I'm doing a check to see if the last storm did any damage to the hedges and fencing." Andie shushed Rupert, who'd wagged his tail excitedly. "Maybe the fresh air will get your creative juices flowing."

"Not sure there's any left to flow." Doc removed his reading glasses and rubbed his eyes tiredly. Rupert came over to rest his head on Doc's knee. "Now, how can I refuse your scruffy face?"

The M & M Farm had a decent amount of land. Not the largest in the area, certainly, probably the smallest when Doc thought about it. But there was enough to make it a lot of work for one person to keep up with.

In the summer, Andie hired a few teenagers from the nearby village to help with the polytunnels. The farm did enough to sustain itself. A good thing, since she seemed to throw herself into the endeavour.

Grabbing his jacket from the hook by the door, Doc followed Andie outside into the beautiful, bright sunlight. A lovely, crisp February morning. The wind had finally died down. He chuckled when Rupert took off at a mad dash, racing around after nothing at all.

"What did you feed him this morning?"

"My Rups always loves days like this." Andie shrugged. She peered over at him. "How goes the writing?"

"Shite."

"That good?" Andie gave him what he thought might be a sympathetic smile. He wasn't sure. "We're not distracting you, are we?"

"A speck of dust is distracting at the moment. You're the least of my worries when it comes to my writing," Doc assured her quickly. He enjoyed her company, probably too much. "Inspiration has been a fleeting mistress in the past year. I've gone all over the world trying to hunt some down."

"Maybe you have to let the inspiration find you?"

"Maybe." Doc didn't exactly know how inspiration would find him. It certainly hadn't in the past twelve months. "I'm beating my head against my laptop at the moment."

"Careful. You might hurt something important."

"Not literally.... Ah. You were joking." Doc shook his head and chuckled wryly. "I could bash my head against the wall, and I'm not sure it would make a difference."

"Just don't mess up your glasses. I like the way you look in them." Andie sent another grin his way before picking up the pace to catch up to Rupert.

Watching the two playfully chase each other, Doc allowed the sun and crisp air to wake him up a little. He thought once the weather warmed up more, maybe he'd take his laptop outside to write. If nothing else, it would be a lovely view.

The farm was beautiful.

Andie was beautiful.

Stop thinking about Andie.

"Is the water tank that interesting?"

Doc jolted out of his thoughts when Andie called out to him. He realised he'd been staring at one of the farm's rainwater collection systems. "Fascinating."

"Sure. Maybe I should've pulled you away from the computer sooner?" she teased when he caught up to her. "Not much of a walk if you stand and admire the farm equipment for most of it."

They meandered along the path that skirted the edges of the orchard. It was small in comparison to many he'd seen, but enough to have a good yield each year.

"Are you still trading with other local farms?"

"Don't think I've bought much at the shops in ages. Trade my fruit for veggies, dairy, and even some meat. It's not a bad way of doing business, since I sell the bulk of the fruit to Ainsley, who makes a variety of spreads with it." Andie paused to check the base of one of the apple trees. "These go to the brewery across the county for their cider."

"Clever."

"I have my moments." Andie moved on to a second tree. "Saves me from having to come up with ways to use them."

Doc couldn't help watching her intently while she inspected several trees in the orchard. She was so methodical in her care of the farm. And beautiful. It made his chest ache in a way that confused him.

There was a comfort to being home in Scotland. Doc had genuinely hoped the distance might dull his feelings. It hadn't.

His connection to her hadn't snapped in their absence. It had strengthened... in his heart, at least. He had no idea if she felt anything for him at all aside from maybe being hurt over his abrupt departure.

"You okay?" Andie was glancing over her shoulder at him.

"Fine." He rubbed his fist over his chest a few times, trying to ease the weirdness away. "How are the roots?"

"Solid."

Late in the afternoon, Doc sat outside with Andie. They'd built a little bonfire in one of the tilled fields. She'd made them a gourmet hot chocolate and fresh-baked fruit tartlets.

They sat on little seats made out of tree trunks. Doc sipped hot chocolate and watched the sunset. The day had been a glorious one.

The bright blue sky slowly grew darker. He watched the golden sun's rays dip lower and lower before disappearing over the mountains in the distance. Clouds diffused some of the colours, creating a riot of shades of dark blue, purple, and pink.

"Not a bad life."

Doc glanced over at Andie before turning back to the sunset. "No, not at all."

Chapter 5
Andie

March

"Are you being careful, Da?" Andie paced the kitchen while talking on the phone with both of her parents. "They're talking about a full lockdown in Italy. Do you have food? Masks? Toilet paper? Can I send anything?"

"We're fine, *cara mia*. I promise. We're well-stocked with food," her mother assured her. "We did our monthly shop before they shut everything down. We're fine."

Her parents and grandparents had all gone to a family property. It was secluded. Hopefully, they'd have an extra level of protection, being outside the city.

She was still worried, especially for her grandparents. The virus was spreading. Everything changed on a daily basis, it seemed.

No one knew what might happen. Andie struggled between wanting to stay informed and not losing herself in the constant news cycle. It was a blessing that the farm kept her from simply scrolling on her phone endlessly.

"How is Docherty doing?" Her father was the one who brought the subject back around to her guest at the farm. "Behaving himself?"

"Da," Andie grumbled. "When has he ever not behaved himself?"

"Pity. You'd make such a handsome couple," her mother teased.

"Hanging up now. Love you." Andie ended the call with her parents' laughter echoing in her ear. She glanced down at Rupert, who'd pressed himself up against her side. "Can I help you? You've already had your afternoon snack."

Rupert wagged his tail; snack was his second-favourite word. She rolled her eyes at him—her spoiled mutt. He didn't relent.

"Why don't we check on the berries again? Make sure they're getting what they need." Andie found the early stages of spring planting to be the most delicate when using polytunnels. So she had to make sure they got just the right level of care. "Maybe we'll check on Doc. He might need you to cheer him up if words are still being difficult."

Opening the farmhouse door, Andie allowed Rupert to bolt out into the sunlight. She'd had a late lunch. They were a few weeks away from her first harvest of the season; her polytunnel set-up allowed her to have several throughout the year up to around December, if things went well.

Things didn't always go well.

A meow drew her attention to the barn. She checked on her rescued mousers, making sure they had water and food still. They appeared to all be doing well.

"How're things going then?" Andie crouched beside one of her most recent rescues. "See, you've grown all your hair back."

The cat rubbed up against her legs and then meandered back into the shadows of the barn. A quick glance showed their beds, food, and water were all fine. One more thing to check off her long daily to-do list.

It was too early in the season to bring on help. She had at least another month or two for that. If she didn't love the farm so much, it would've also seemed far too daunting to even begin her daily tasks.

They were inching their way into spring. Green was returning, along with all the other wonderful, vibrant colours. It was a lovely time to be outside, even with the occasional drizzle.

"Hello, Rupert. Did you find Doc?" Andie stepped out of the barn to be greeted by a gleefully wagging tail. He dropped a hat at her feet. "Well, you've spotted part of him at least. Where's the rest?"

Rupert dashed between her and the tiny house, trying to hurry her up. He seemed to think he was a sheepdog. And she was obviously his lone ewe.

"Baa." Doc waited for them in the doorway of the little house.

"Hilarious." Andie rolled her eyes at Doc, who laughed in response. She peered down at her happily wagging dog. "I am not a sheep."

"Baa." Doc leaned against the doorframe and smiled at her. "He seems to be herding you like his lost lamb."

It made his eyes crinkle. A dimple showed on his cheek. Andie sternly reminded her heart not to do anything foolish, like fall any further in love with him.

Andie couldn't help returning his smile. Some of her worries faded away. "Up for an afternoon walk?"

"I've been waiting for you." Doc stepped forward, shutting the door behind him. "I managed a hundred words."

"Brilliant."

"Then deleted them."

"Less brilliant." Andie sent Rupert chasing after his ball down the lane. "You can always try again later."

Over the last few weeks, they'd trekked all over the farm and surrounding countryside. Each afternoon they set off in a different direction. Time always flew by while they chatted about everything and nothing.

It was comfortable. Familiar. Andie felt like she'd rediscovered her most comfortable and warm cardigan. And she was terrified to let it (him) go.

Not again.

He might not come back.

Andie worried about that a lot since his return. He'd been chased off once already. "Doc? Are you comfortable here?"

"I'm happy." He patted Rupert on the head, then wandered on down the path.

Happy is good.

"Your hat." Andie offered it to him. "Not sure how Rupert managed to snag it from you."

"I made the mistake of leaving it within reach." Doc glanced over at her. "Maybe you're not feeding him enough."

"He gets more than enough." Andie kicked a pebble on the path. "You sure you're happy? I'm not bothering you?"

"Yes, I'm happy. No, you haven't bothered me." Doc was his usual blunt self. He shoved his hands into his pockets. "Is it my face?"

"I like your face. It's not your face," Andie quickly assured him. "Just want you to be comfortable."

"I am. More than I've been in quite a long time."

Chapter 6
Doc

April

Spring had arrived. Things hadn't changed much on the farm. The world seemed to be coming to a complete standstill around them.

Everything was slowly growing greener. The weather had warmed up a little. Daffodils were blooming. It all felt fresh and inviting; they continued to enjoy their daily walks.

Andie spoke with her family every day. She was concerned about the situation in Italy. He couldn't blame her.

In Scotland, they were isolated on the farm. A small measure of comfort for them. A mercy compared to what others were experiencing.

Several of the local farms had come together to set up a trading system of sorts. Eggs for produce. Produce for milk and cheese from the dairy across the county. It kept the larder full of more than just berries when getting into the village seemed less than ideal.

A scratching at the door broke Doc out of his thoughts. He abandoned his blank page and went to let Rupert inside. The Airedale danced around him, then began head-butting the back of his legs.

"Are you sure you're not a sheepdog? Where are we going, eh?" Doc allowed himself to be pushed outside. He followed Rupert across the farm into the orchard, where he found a ladder on the ground and Andie clinging to the branches of an apple tree. "What's your next trick going to be? Levitation?"

"I will throw apples at you."

Laughing to himself, Doc grabbed the ladder and propped it up against the tree. He held onto it while she clambered down from her perch. She shifted the ladder to yet another tree.

"What are you doing?" Doc held the ladder while she climbed up it.

"Checking to see if they're doing all right." Andie came back down the ladder and turned to lean against it. "Not really necessary at this stage. They won't be ripe for picking until late in the summer. I just... want a good harvest this year. Something good to come of this year."

"They'll do brilliantly. I'm sure. More fruitful than my attempts at writing have been." Doc patted her shoulder awkwardly. "How can I help?"

"You can let go of the ladder." Andie tried to take it from him. "I can manage."

"Sure. But maybe I need some time outside."

"To evade your deadline?" Andie smiled when he grumbled under his breath. "Wasn't the fresh Scottish air supposed to get the words flowing?"

"Supposed. No guarantees. Writing can be like farming. We don't always get a harvest from the seeds of creativity we plant." Doc sighed. He carried the ladder and followed her through the orchard. "Fairly confident my words have abandoned me for the moment."

"I'll buy you a thesaurus for your birthday." Andie pointed to another tree. "Prop it up there for me, please?"

"What are you looking for?"

"Signs of trouble. I had to remove a few trees two years ago when they developed issues. I'm paranoid about it happening again." She clambered up the rungs and began inspecting the tree.

"Overly cautious." He understood her fear. The farm wasn't massive, and losses could easily stack up into something unmanageable.

"Not sure there's a difference." She finished her inspection and returned to the ground. "Think we've nothing to worry about this year. Everything seems good. A pity, since we've all gone into lockdown. Who knows if I'll even be able to sell much?"

"Think it'll put that much of a damper on your year?"

"I think we're all in for a dreadfully different year than expected." Andie grabbed the ladder and began carrying it back through the orchard. "Too early to say more than that. Truthfully? I'm not sure it'll affect the demand for fruit, but the logistics of delivery might become tricky. I'm trying not to just assume the worst, which is hard."

Following her over to the barn, Doc watched her struggle a little with the ladder when Rupert decided to grab onto one of the rungs. It was hard to tell if the dog wanted to help or play fetch. He couldn't help laughing at her predicament.

"Rups. Stop it." Andie settled the ladder on the ground with a little difficulty while trying not to laugh herself. "It is not a stick to fetch, you absolute numpty."

"From his perspective, it's many sticks to fetch." Doc chuckled. He stepped closer to her. "Sure I can't help?"

The words were just out of his mouth when Rupert yanked particularly hard, and Andie wound up flat on her back with the ladder over her. She laughed when her dog immediately leapt into the fray. Doc crouched down to attempt to help her up.

"Are you okay?"

"Managed to catch it with my arms, so I imagine I'll have some bruises. Thank goodness I've got a newer ladder and not the heavy, wooden monstrosity my granddad used to use." Andie laughed when Rupert tried to grab the ladder again.

He gently herded Rupert out of his way and then tried to lift the ladder off her. It didn't help that Andie couldn't stop giggling. "Maybe I should write about a hapless farmer and her excitable companion."

"We'd give you plenty of fodder for the novel." Andie took his hand and sat up. Her fingers flexed against his palm before pulling out of his grasp. "My excitement for the day is officially over. Care for a cuppa? I could use some caffeine to get me through the rest of my to-do list."

They managed to get the ladder into the barn

without much problem. Rupert seemed oddly fixated on it. Doc tried not to think about her hand in his, her fingers grazing against his palm.

His writer's retreat had transformed into a slow form of emotional torture. Of being within reach of something precious. And not allowing himself to go for it.

Self-preservation or self-flagellation?

It was difficult to tell.

"You coming with or going to stare at the splotch of red paint on the barn a bit more?" Andie drew him out of his thoughts. She waited patiently by the barn door while he'd clearly drifted off in his thoughts.

"Sorry. Contemplating my novel." Doc grimaced at the attempt to divert the conversation. "Or the lack of it."

"Words will come."

"Will they?" Doc dragged his hand roughly through his hair. "I might turn all the way grey before I type 'the end.'"

"Makes you look ruggedly distinguished." She winked at him before jogging toward the cottage with Rupert on her heels. "Tea's waiting."

And so is my soon-to-be re-broken heart.

Chapter 7
Andie

May

THE WORLD HAD WELL AND TRULY SHUT DOWN. Andie had thrown herself into farm projects. Ones she'd put at the bottom of her extensive to-do list.

It kept her mind off worrying about her family in Italy.

Doc spent most of his time grumbling into a mug of coffee in front of his laptop. She didn't know how much progress he'd made on his novel. Being in Scotland hadn't seemed to break through his writer's block like he'd hoped.

For all her initial concerns, Andie was grateful to have a companion who did more than wag his tail and bark at her when she spoke. Doc made early morning breakfasts and late evening suppers bearable. Less lonely than she would have otherwise felt.

"Easy, Rups." Andie placed a hand on her excited dog's head. He wiggled around her, wagging his tail wildly. "All right. We'll walk down the lane to the gate. C'mon."

Pushing the heavy-duty cart stacked with crates of fruit, Andie made her way down the long driveway leading to the gate by the road into the village. Each morning she set out the containers for pick up by the other local farms or the nearby brewery.

She couldn't drive around to drop them off and have a natter like she used to do. So they'd worked out a system that kept all of them far apart. They often left supplies for her in return.

An odd sort of bartering system that made her chuckle and left her feeling grateful for her community.

There was a box waiting at the little drop-off point at the end of the lane. She'd built it with recycled lumber from an ongoing shed project. The small stand provided shelter from wind and rain while keeping the crates safe off the ground until they were picked up.

"We've got treats, Rups. Even one for you." Andie grabbed the bag of biscuits off the top and tossed one to him. "Your auntie Mariah made them especially for you."

Mariah ran a food shop in the village. They'd been best friends since primary school, so Andie was relieved to see a letter poking out from one side of the box.

"News from the outside world." Andie carried the box back down the lane with Rupert barking madly beside her, clearly wanting a second of the home-baked treats. "You're not a hobbit. You don't get a second breakfast."

Once they made it to the cottage, Andie checked out the contents of the package. Aside from the treats for Rupert, there were scones, a pot of jam, a couple books, the letter, and a packet of biscuits definitely meant for Doc. She decided to take them out to him.

"Why don't we see how Doc's writer's block is going?" She laughed when Rupert immediately whipped around in a circle. "Yes, we're going to see your best friend."

The writer's block wasn't going well. She found Doc on the floor, on his back with his eyes closed. A pen and several crushed sheets of paper surrounded him.

"A very odd sort of a séance. Who are you attempting to contact? Hemmingway or Austen?" Andie nudged his leg gently with her foot. She snickered when Rupert pounced on him. She pulled her phone out and got a photo of him. "I call this *A Vision of a Tormented Artist at Work*. It's a little long for a title, but it really encompasses the meaning."

"Artist?"

"You paint with ink and paper. And words, some days. Maybe not recently," Andie teased. She collected the crumpled balls and dropped them in the rubbish bin. "Marian sent a packet of your favourite biscuits."

Doc opened one eye to see her waving the packet over his head. "I was communing with the blank page."

"Right."

"Attempting to flow with the emptiness."

"Right." Andie drew the word out. "Poetic way of saying you've written sod all?"

"Rude but accurate." Doc covered his face with his arm. "Are you here to do more than laugh in the face of my failure?"

"Biscuit delivery." She set the packet on the table out of reach of Rupert's curious snout. "I'm clearing a section of the field at the northern end of the farm today. I want to get a head start on putting in new polytunnels and a proper greenhouse. So I'll be there most of the day. Taking a sandwich and thermos for myself. The cottage is open if you get hungry. And I've got my phone."

"I'll be here. On the floor. Dramatically avoiding Microsoft Word and contemplating death by paper cut." Doc opened both eyes and grinned up at her.

Andie flushed, looking away from the boyish grin, dimples, and the little wrinkles around his blue eyes. "I'll... Well, I. Okay. See you later."

Oh, yes.

Way to play it cool and collected. He's definitely going to notice your absolute inability to be normal. Oh my god. Why am I so useless? Kill me now.

Preferably not with paper cuts.

She wanted to kiss him again. Being hopelessly in love with an old friend was almost a tragedy. She worried about losing his friendship.

She was worried about whether he'd understand kissing was all she'd ever be interested in.

That was a problem for another day.

In an ordinary world, Andie probably would've hired someone to come and clear out the portion of the paddock for the tunnels and greenhouse. She could manage it on her own. Unfortunately, it was going to take a lot longer. It had originally been home to her gran's two horses, but there hadn't been any on the farm in decades. Andie wanted to use the paddock for something better. A few rows of the arched tunnels would make much better use of the land.

"What do you think, Rupert?" Andie glanced at the skip she'd driven out to the site with her little tractor. She planned to spend the day filling it with the timbers and other refuse. "Think we can manage this by the end of the day?"

Rupert lay down in the grass and plopped his head down between his paws. A definite no. Andie set her bag with food on a nearby crate and got to work.

Time flew by while Andie worked. Finally, she clambered up onto a section of the old barn. It allowed her to toss pieces of wood and other trash into the skip.

"Fancy some help?" Doc's voice startled her. She stumbled backward, only to be caught in his arms. "Hello."

"Ciao." She couldn't help grinning up at him.

They were smiling. Then as if pulled by a

magnet, their lips met. This kiss was no less meaningful than the first.

Andie couldn't help sighing against his lips. "Please don't run across the globe this time."

"Can't. We're in a pandemic." Doc chuckled before helping her stand up. "We should talk."

Chapter 8
Doc

May

SHITE.

He'd done it again. Kissed her. Spontaneously. He'd walked out to the paddock to help clear the partially demolished barn. Snogging hadn't been on the agenda.

Her smile had drawn him in, and her laugh when he'd caught her. Her beautiful eyes sparkled in the sunlight. Words might have abandoned him, but his feelings for Andie hadn't.

Conflicting feelings had been what sent him on his worldwide writing tour. Though neither writing nor forgetting had happened. He thought maybe they both needed to talk.

"Doc?" Andie offered him a pair of gloves. "Give me a hand with this beam? Think it might've been part of the load-bearing wall in the barn."

"You might be right. It's large enough." Doc pulled the gloves on. He eyed the beam, trying to decide if the two of them could even manage to lift it without breaking their backs. "Always important to have a good solid base to keep a building standing."

"A building. A relationship. A barn." Andie laughed when he rolled his eyes and sighed dramatically. "How bad is your writing slump to bring you to voluntarily help me with a rubbish pile?"

A fair but harsh assumption. He did have a deadline. One he'd watched go by several times already.

"Less about writing, more about wanting to be outdoors and spend time with you." Doc wondered if he'd been too honest. He could never tell what a neurotypical might find too blunt. He tested the weight of the beam, giving one end a lift. "How did you plan on carrying this on your own?"

"I'd figure it out." Andie had been studiously avoiding his gaze. Finally, she peered over at her dog. "Rups might help."

"Rupert isn't a pack mule."

The dog in question rolled around in the grass in response. Doc chuckled. He laughed harder when

Rupert sneezed loudly and seemed to go back to napping.

"Doc?"

"Hmm?" He paused while bending down to scratch Rupert's belly and went to help her instead. They managed with a lot of effort to drag the beam toward the skip. He had to take a moment to stretch his back out when they'd finished. It was now or never. He had to say what he'd been practising on his walk over. "I'm not sorry I kissed you. Either time. I do regret leaving. Conversations aren't always easy for me."

"And now?"

"Still not easy." Doc busied himself by brushing some dirt off his jeans. "I'm too old to run from things that I find difficult."

"Not sure what your empty manuscript would say in response." Andie laughed while she chucked what looked like a few rusted tools into the tip. "Fancy a cup of tea and a biscuit? I brought a snack with me."

"A biscuit to soothe my wounded author pride?"

Andie seemed to turn contemplative after a moment of watching him. She shaded her eyes from the sun with her hand. "I wish you'd stayed."

Doc sighed deeply. "So do I."

Regret never solved much of anything in his mind. He'd wasted too much time already, bouncing around aimlessly, trying to talk himself out of his feelings. And maybe away from hers. Absence had served only to make his heart confused.

His fondness for her had never changed.

"I didn't mind the kiss. I enjoyed it. Both times." Andie grabbed a thermos out of the bag she'd brought with her to the barn site. She poured tea and offered him the first sip. "We'll have to share."

"But?"

"Not a but so much as a clarification."

"Been cracking open the thesaurus you're giving me as a present so I can remember all my words?" Doc teased. He tried to lighten the conversation a little, but it was hard to keep his mind from shutting down on him. He wanted to have a complete talk with her. To be able to listen and absorb her thoughts and be capable of responding without needing time to process. "What's the clarification?"

"We've never talked about sex."

Doc choked on the tea he'd just drunk. He turned his head away from her and coughed a few times, trying to clear his throat. "All right."

"You know I've dated."

"I'm aware." Doc had hoped for her happiness

while admitting to himself he'd felt a small measure of envy each time.

"I've never really come out to my family. My dates have always known if things progressed into anything even slightly serious. My friends know." Andie reached down to scratch Rupert when he trotted over to lean against her, likely sensing her unease. "I'm asexual."

"Okay."

"I enjoy kissing. I experience love. I'm mad about cuddling. But I've no interest in sex. Never been sexually attracted to someone." Andie trailed off when she glanced at him. "Doc?"

"It has a name." Doc closed his eyes while everything in his mind seemed to spin around like a whirling dervish before slamming to a halt. It was too much to process. All those questions. They had answers. They had a word. A definition. "Oh."

"What?"

"How I feel. It has a name. Asexuality." Doc had struggled with a sense of being abnormal for a lot of his life. Society tended to reinforce that. Being autistic certainly played a part for him, but so did his sexuality, particularly as he got older. "You're going to laugh."

"I won't. Though, maybe a bit of research, since there's an entire spectrum."

"It doesn't always occur to me to do research about how I feel." Doc shrugged. He couldn't shake the sense of awkward anxiety. He didn't really have any idea what words were coming out of his mouth. His mind had stopped processing. "To be honest, I'm never a hundred percent certain how I'm feeling in the first place with just about everything. Sexuality included. I imagine I'll find myself somewhere on that spectrum."

"You enjoyed the kissing?"

"I did." He grabbed a couple of biscuits from the packet she held out. "But I didn't want more."

"From the kissing or me?"

"From the kissing," Doc rushed to clarify. "We've danced around our feelings for each other. But I've never been interested in sex—or attracted to someone that way. I've had romantic thoughts about you."

"Danced round though never quite to the same rhythm." Andie hopped up to sit on a crate beside him. "We're stuck on the farm for the time being. Nothing to prevent us from figuring things out together."

"I've been told I'm bad at relationships."

"Or maybe you've spent most of your relationships trying to be someone else? Trying to be what a lot of society thinks we should be?" Andie tossed a toy from her pocket across the field. Rupert was off like a rocket after it. "Who says you can't evaluate things for yourself? Decide for yourself?"

She made an excellent point. They weren't going anywhere anytime soon. And writing clearly wasn't going to happen if he tried to force it.

"Can you be patient with me while I'm figuring it out?" Doc bent down to grab the ball Rupert dropped at his feet. He launched it across the paddock. "Off you go, Rups."

"I'll do you one better." Andie slid closer and placed a hand on his arm. "We can figure it out together."

Rupert spat the toy out at his feet. Doc sent him racing after it once again. The dog did a brilliant job of releasing tension from difficult moments in the conversation, if nothing else.

"Give me a hand with more of the timber. I made enough sandwiches for two. We can have a late lunch, then go for a walk." Andie glanced around at the barn. "I've made a surprising amount of progress for one morning."

"In more ways than one." Doc got to his feet and surveyed the area with her. "I thought you'd gotten someone to demolish it and handle removing the remnants."

"I had. They did the demolition for the most part but wound up not being able to finish. They'd planned to come back in a month or so." Andie gestured around at the piles of rubbish. "Not sure when that'll happen, given the state of the world at large. If I can fill up the skip, maybe I can have them pick it up and empty it. Save some money and give me something to do as well."

"You can reuse some of the wood. It's not all rotted out."

"I've thought about it. Some of it I can use while setting up the polytunnels. A lot of it's ruined, though. Better off not to start with a faulty foundation. I'd only wind up doing triple the work and likely the cost at replacing things for a second time." Andie launched what looked like a horseshoe at the skip. "I'm keeping everything I can recycle on this trailer. I've got a tarp to put over it once we're finished."

They worked for another hour before deciding to call it quits. Doc enjoyed sharing her packed lunch. They found a nice shady spot under one of the large trees to eat.

It was *almost* a date. Almost. Not enough to

make him nervous about messing everything up again but enough to seem more than just sandwiches with friends.

Societal niceties had always been a confusing muddle for him. He'd leaned into the reclusive author mystique the older he'd gotten. It made for a brilliant excuse to avoid situations where he felt doomed to fail from the start.

If no one expected him to be chatty or charming, he wouldn't have to put on the mask. To play pretend. Part of what made him fall in love with Andie was she'd never needed the façade.

She was as comfortable in the silence as she was in talking about the most mundane things. None of it mattered to her. She simply enjoyed his company.

Hard not to fall in love with that.

Andie tapped his hand, offering him one of the two water bottles she'd brought with her. "Not a bad spot for a first impromptu date."

"Not bad at all." Doc had to chuckle. He'd missed how often they seemed to almost be able to read each other's minds. "I'll even walk you home when we're finished."

"And kiss me at my door?"

"After we've eaten sandwiches with pickled onions and cheese?" Doc managed to maintain a straight face before they both dissolved into laughter. "Maybe after you brush your teeth."

"Have you tried writing a book of jokes to cure your block?"

Doc gave her a wounded look, clutching at his chest while she continued to laugh. "Way to hit where it hurts the most."

Chapter 9
Andie

June

IT IS TIME TO WAKE UP.

You are one with the flow of the universe.

It is time to wake up.

"Bugger off." Andie searched blindly for her phone before finding it underneath the book she'd been reading late into the night. "Why do I still have this sodding app in the first place?"

Neither Rupert nor her phone had an answer for her. Finally, Andie rolled out of bed. She wanted to get down to the paddock early and look at it with fresh eyes.

Three weeks of back-breaking work had cleared the barn and paddock out completely. It had taken two trips to get rid of everything. Her friend at the brewery down the road intended to recycle the wood for some project of his own.

It took longer to get the bathroom door open than it did to shower. Some mornings it was stiffer than her joints. She finally managed to lift it slightly, then twist it slowly enough, and it swung open.

"You are my next project." She glowered ominously at it.

Splashing water onto her face, Andie quickly got ready for her day. She dragged on a cardigan and dungarees. Her boots waited by the back door.

She paused to flip on the coffee machine. It would have the nectar of the gods ready for her by the time she returned from the paddock. Rupert danced around excitedly while she tugged on her boots.

"Ready for a quick walk?" Andie laughed when he wagged even more enthusiastically. "All right."

She grabbed a flapjack from the traybake she'd made the night before. Something to tide her over before she made a full breakfast. Her mind had been spinning all night with ideas for the paddock.

"What do you think, Rupert?" Andie stood at the gate leading into the old paddock. She'd brought her tractor in to mow the grass and prepare the space for the polytunnels. If the weather held out, she wanted to start constructing them today or tomorrow. "Not bad, is it?"

It usually required several pairs of hands to get them set up. Andie hoped Doc would be all the help needed. Rupert didn't exactly have the capacity to do much other than cheer her up if she got frustrated.

Or... when she got frustrated.

Even with buying the DIY kits, putting together the larger tunnels took a lot of effort. She'd had a few collapse on her previously. There'd been a lot of cursing that day.

"A farmer in her field surveying the land." Doc joined her at the gate. He offered a mug of coffee; he'd obviously stopped at the cottage before coming to find her. "I managed half a page last night."

"Did you?"

"I even kept most of it." Doc had begun growing out his beard a little bit. Andie thought it made him look like a weather-hardened sea captain. "My editor will be thrilled if I manage a full page at some point."

"See? Maybe Scotland has been good for your writer's block." Andie hoped his luck continued to improve. It hurt to see him stymied when she knew what a brilliant author he was. "You'll get there."

Doc grumbled into his coffee and leaned his

elbows against the gate. "I'd prefer to get there faster, if at all possible."

"Wouldn't we all?" Andie certainly wouldn't have minded if the tunnels put themselves up.

The polytunnel kits were still sitting in the barn on the other side of the property. Andie found it useful to visualise where she wanted them before starting. It gave her an idea of what she wanted. She hoped to have more planting capacity and maybe even room for a second shed or even a tiny cottage like the one Doc currently called home.

She gave the paddock one last look. "Have you had breakfast yet? I've a mind to cook something up."

"Not going to try to survive on coffee alone?" He took a sip from his mug. "I could eat."

"Come on then. Bacon and eggs should do nicely. The last food delivery had a nice packet of bacon." Andie whistled for Rupert, who'd gone flying across the paddock at top speed. He caught up to them while they returned to the cottage. "Italy's opening back up."

"So are we. A little."

The easing of restrictions scared Andie. She didn't know if she was ready for things to return to some semblance of normal. It felt a little too optimistic; not for the first time, she was grateful they lived more remotely than most.

"How are your parents doing?"

"They've been experimenting with baking bread and making wine." Andie shook her head, laughing. She'd already promised to crate up some of her berry harvest to ship out to her parents. "You can take the farmer away from the farm, but they're never going to be satisfied with remaining still for too long. Da's apparently been alphabetising her cookbooks. She's banned him from touching them."

"What's wrong with alphabetising books?"

"Nothing, if he'd stuck with the authors' names or the book titles. He came up with some bizarre system of his own." Andie snickered. "She still hasn't quite figured out what, and since he's banned, he won't tell her. I think maybe they've been stuck indoors for too long."

"Your parents have always been unique." Doc joined her in laughing. He reached out to pluck a stray leaf out of her hair. "I'm glad they're doing okay."

Nodding in agreement, Andie tried not to blush. It wasn't like her. The blushing. She thought they'd gotten past that stage.

There were still moments when she expected

him to bolt away from her. Run across the globe again. He hadn't thus far.

But the remembered pain still lingered.

Her fingers brushed against his hand while they walked side by side. She risked a peek at him out of her the corner of her eye. No response. Nothing at all.

It didn't necessarily mean anything. Doc often appeared like a closed book when it came to reacting emotionally. Things often bubbled under the surface that she couldn't see.

He took time to process things. Andie knew he'd begun researching asexuality. She'd promised herself that she'd be patient with him.

They'd get there. He just required time to filter through everything in his mind. She knew he'd get there eventually.

Andie grazed her fingers against the back of his hand for a second time, then slipped her hand into his. "Going to be a lovely summer day, isn't it? Think we might get some rain toward the end of the week. I can smell it in the air."

"You can't." Doc didn't so much as blink at their holding hands. A first for them. "Not even Rupert's nose is good enough to scent rain days in advance."

"The nose knows." Andie tapped her nose and

grinned when he grumbled at her ridiculousness. "Think I'll get the frame for the first tunnel up this afternoon once I've finished all my morning tasks."

"Want a hand?"

"I've got one." She lifted up their joined hands. "An extra one at that."

"You obviously need more coffee. Your jokes have gotten worse." Doc dodged out of the way when Rupert barrelled between them, chasing after a bee. "You won't enjoy getting stung if you catch it."

"No sense of self-preservation." Andie couldn't help wondering if it was a trait Rupert had gotten from her. She was definitely opening her heart up to be broken once again. "And yes, I could use help. Rups isn't so good at holding things up for me."

"The lack of opposable thumbs?"

"I'm sure that's part of it. Also, a tendency to run off with anything even potentially resembling a stick." Andie whistled for Rupert when he went to chase off down the lane. "Rups? It's not time to check for a drop-off. We're having breakfast."

Leading the way into the cottage, Andie went straight into the kitchen. She melted a healthy portion of butter in a pan and then tossed in some leftover boiled potatoes. Doc helped her dice up some onion and peppers to go with it, along with slices of bacon.

It didn't take long for them to have a delicious breakfast hash and perfectly buttered toast. She tried not to think about how he knew exactly how she liked her bread toasted and buttered. It was sweet that he remembered.

Stop blushing over toast.

I'm being weird and ridiculous.

Chapter 10
Doc

July

THE WORLD HAD BEGUN TO OPEN UP AGAIN, AND Doc didn't know whether to be pleased or sad. Finally, they'd be able to stray from the farm. The past few months had flown by for him when he thought about Andie.

When his mind turned to his writing, Doc thought time had crawled at whatever was slower than a snail's pace. Sloth? Inchworm? Paint drying? He tried to reel his mind back in when a thousand other ideas flew out. If only words on the page could come as quickly as random thoughts in his head.

He had a million words chaotically floating around in his mind until he tried to put pen to paper.

And then he conveniently forgot all of them aside from "the," which he typed and deleted repeatedly. He didn't believe in purgatory or limbo, but this was definitely an author's version of it.

A bark outside drew his attention from his empty cup of tea and the blank page in front of him. Rupert, which meant Andie. He dragged his fingers roughly through his greying hair, trying to appear like he hadn't stumbled from the bed to the coffee maker to the desk without a comb or a splash of water on his face.

I'm going to chase her off before we've even done more than dip our toes in the water of what this could be between us.

She'd been so patient with him. Doc had gone a little blank when they'd talked about asexuality. It had taken him a while to unravel his thoughts—to pull apart some of the almost painful moments from the past where he'd wondered if he was broken.

He couldn't rush. No matter how much his heart wanted him to. He'd read everything he could find online about the spectrum of asexuality.

It fit.

It was the only thing that had fit him.

"Rough morning?" Andie grinned at him after taking in his plaid pyjama bottoms, sock-covered feet, and his Pink Floyd T-shirt. "I ventured far from home."

"Drove into the village?"

"Fine, fine. Take all the adventure away from me. Rups and I went into the village to make sure it still existed. It does. Picked up some dark chocolate and cherry scones at the bakery. Want to share? I've already got coffee brewing." Andie waved the bag in front of him. "How are the words going this morning?"

"Going anywhere but where I want them."

Andie's gaze drifted down to his feet and back up again. "Why don't we have a snack here? I can bring the coffee over. The rain has left the farm a wee bit muddy. Not sure you want to trek around out there in your socks."

"I have shoes." Doc gestured to his boots and wellies near the door. "Several pairs, in fact."

"I like your feet."

"Weird, but thank you." Doc never knew how to graciously accept a compliment. No matter what it was about. He pulled on his wellies. "How was the world out there?"

"Odd." Andie waited patiently until he was ready to go. She glanced down at Rupert, who raced around in the yard. "What are the chances he allows me to wipe his paws?"

"Slim to none?" Doc laughed when the Airedale threw himself down to roll around in the mud. "Not sure it's the paws you should be worried about."

"Rupert." Andie shoved the bag into Doc's hands and raced after her dog. "No, you bloody mutt, I'm not playing chase. Come back here. Rups."

Doc laughed so hard that he had to grab onto a nearby post for support. She was so bright and beautiful and cheerful. "Need a hand?"

"Just keep the scones safe." Andie finally managed to grab hold of her dog. "You're having a bath, Rups. I'm not letting you drag mud all over the cottage because you had to roll around in it. Honestly."

"Why don't you rinse him off outside, and I'll grab a towel from the cottage for you?" Doc followed her toward the farmhouse. "You have a special one for him?"

"Large, ratty beach towel. It's on the chair in the bathroom. I'd planned to give him a proper bath later." Andie tsked while struggling to keep a hold of Rupert. "Honestly. What am I going to do with you? You've more mud than fur at the moment, I swear. Were you hoping for a spa day?"

Leaving Andie to lecture her poor dog, Doc made his way into the house. He left the bag of scones in the kitchen and then made his way through to the bathroom. It took a second to wiggle the door open; he found the towel draped over the back of a rickety old wooden chair.

Doc returned to find Andie chasing Rupert around with the garden hose. "Not sure he wants to wash away his mud mask."

"Give me a hand, will you?" Andie huffed with frustrated laughter. "Don't frown at me, Rups. I'm not torturing you."

The frenzied wiggling from Rupert definitely seemed to indicate torment was happening. Doc left the towel by the door and went to help. Andie's jeans and Nirvana T-shirt were mussed with some of the mud from her dog.

Doc stepped forward and got a face full of water and dirt when Rupert shook his fur. "I left my manuscript for this."

"Is it a manuscript when it's blank?"

"You wound me." Doc sighed dramatically. He went bravely into the breach, grasping at the wiggling Rupert to hold him steady. "The beast is under control."

"Did you and Rupert come together to be overly

dramatic for my benefit?" Andie dragged a hand through her messed-up hair, shoving the wet locks out of her face. She aimed the water at Rupert, who tried to break free. "I promise to give you all the treats if you let me get this mud off you."

Rupert finally settled down. Doc kept hold of him while Andie rinsed him off. He waited until she'd turned the water off to reach back to grab the towel.

They managed to dry Rupert off and guide him into the house before he could take off for the mud once again. Andie leaned wearily against Doc. They both laughed at the state of their muddy clothing.

"Not sure I want to rinse myself off in the same manner." Doc helped her wind the garden hose back up. "Why don't we both get changed? And I'll meet you back here for... delayed scones and coffee?"

Trudging carefully through the muck, Doc managed to make it to the tiny cottage unscathed. He changed into clean jeans and a shirt. Since the wellies were already muddy, he decided to wear them again.

The path certainly hadn't improved magically in the five minutes it had taken him to change. Rupert greeted him at the farmhouse door. Doc had to block his escape while squeezing inside.

"Aren't you too old to be such a menace?" Doc gave Rupert a good scratch and then followed the dog into the kitchen, where a tired Andie was slumped into a chair with a mug clutched in her hands. "Still not a morning person?"

"Nonna keeps conning me into trying these 'better sleep' apps on my phone. I've had nightmares about joining meditation cults. It's not helping." Andie groaned dramatically. "I can't figure out how to delete the sodding thing off my phone for the life of me. It's possessed."

"The app or your phone?"

"Both." Andie slid her phone across the table to him when he motioned for it. "I'm begging for divine intervention at this point."

"Not a deity, but I'm a dab hand at removing things from my phone. Amazing what you'll learn when you're procrastinating." Doc found the apps setting on her device and managed to uninstall the meditation one. "There you go. I've freed you from the cult."

"My hero." Andie shoved the bag of scones toward him. "My thanks in baked goods."

"Always happy to be of assistance. With muddy mutts and wayward electronics." Doc relaxed into the chair. He'd forgotten in his travels how easy being around Andie had always been. She was one of the few people who set his mind and anxiety at ease. "I'm glad I came home."

Andie seemed to struggle for a second before smiling brightly. "So am I."

Chapter 11
August

Andie

Waking up without the meditation app proved far more straightforward than Andie expected. She no longer wanted to fling her phone across the room. Instead, a simple alarm did the job far better—and she'd stopped dreaming about cults.

A definite added bonus.

"You ready, Rup?" Andie peered down at her wagging Airedale. "Long day in the fields for us. Well, the tunnels."

Rupert danced around in the kitchen while Andie chugged down the last of her coffee. They hadn't seen Doc that morning. She hoped words had started flowing for him.

August and September were often the busiest times of year for Andie, so she'd brought in a couple of the local teenagers who'd helped her the last few summers. They worked for a couple of hours each, staggered times to keep all of them safe.

It was better than nothing, though not as much help as she was used to. She usually had three or four of them working several hours every day during the summer. The pandemic had made life a little more complicated.

"It could always be worse, eh, Rups?" Rupert dashed over to her, leaning against her legs while she scratched the top of his head. "At least I have you all the time."

And Doc.

Maybe he'll stay this time around.

Her plans for the old paddock had begun to take shape. The entire old barn had been removed finally, and she'd built her shed with Doc's help as well as getting the polytunnels up. Planting hadn't begun, but she'd save that for later in the year.

The world continued to open up more and more. Her parents had talked about coming to visit. Andie cautioned them to wait a little longer. When it came to health, better to be safe than sorry, but she did miss them immeasurably.

Summer had kept her busy, thankfully. Maybe not quite as in previous years, but not enough to sink the farm. They would all persevere.

"How goes the berries?" Doc joined her in one of the polytunnels.

"How goes the writing?" Andie chuckled when he groaned loudly. "Sorry. Are we pretending you're a farmhand today? You've forgotten your dungarees."

"If I wanted harassment, I would've stayed on the group Zoom with my agent and editor. Vicious." Doc plucked one of the strawberries and popped it into his mouth. "I've decided to scrap my idea and start fresh."

"Nothing wrong with a fresh start." Andie handed him an empty bucket. "Try to harvest more than you eat, please."

"I would never." Doc ate another one with a grin before focusing on helping rather than hindering. "Half and half, at least."

They worked in a cheerful sort of silence for several hours. Andie put on a playlist of music—a mixture of both of their favourites while Rupert darted back and forth between them.

The romantic part of Andie's heart, the dreamer in her soul, had always imagined moments like this. She'd fantasized about having someone to share the farm with. She'd never minded being alone, but there was always the hope of more.

A quiet dream Andie had never shared with anyone. And it had always been Doc who she imagined with her. It was everything she dreamt of.

And she was terrified it would end.

Several hours and many full baskets later, Andie had made more progress than anticipated. The extra hands really paid off. She hoped at some point to be able to bring in all of her usual summer helpers; the world being shut down had thrown a spanner in the works.

"When do these get picked up?"

Andie checked her watch. "I'll drive them down to the little stand at the end of the lane now. Wayne from two farms over should be by shortly. They make all sorts of jams. Probably sell a good half of my berries to them through the year."

"Why don't I help you load them up?" Doc grabbed a couple of the baskets. "Is it hard running the farm alone?"

Andie risked a glance over at him. She tightened her hands around the basket handle. "Not alone now, am I?"

"No." Doc followed her out of the tunnel toward

where she'd parked her old tractor with a trailer attached for the baskets. "Not alone."

Rupert, as always, broke up the slight awkwardness that descended. He darted between them, back and forth, in the hopes of a scratch or a treat. Andie laughed and sent him running after the ball she'd kept in her pocket for him.

"Want me to ride up with you?"

"I can manage." Andie waved off the offer. She thought maybe they both needed a second to clear the tension. "Fancy a late lunch?"

"Why don't I make us some sandwiches?" Doc strode quickly toward the house without waiting for an answer.

Andie crouched down when Rupert returned to her. She grabbed the ball and led him toward the tractor. "Up we get."

Rupert had a space all his own on the tractor. Andie forced herself to take a few calming breaths. They were always dancing around each other—a few steps forward and then some more back.

"Ready, Rups?" She smiled when he wagged his tail. "I'm glad someone is feeling enthusiastic."

August days were some of her favourites. Blue skies, fluffy white clouds. Green. Everything seemed bright and lush. Rain was usually limited during the summer.

It was perfect for farming. She often wore tank tops and shorts while outside. It just made for lovely, lazy days even while busy working.

Andie drove down to the end of the lane and parked beside the little stand. She followed Rupert down to the ground. "Want to carry some of these for me?"

Rupert spun around in a circle. Andie took that as a no. She pulled her gloves on and grabbed the first of the crates.

In no time at all, Andie had gotten the stack carefully sorted and ready for pick up. The ride back to the cottage went far too quickly. She wasn't ready to face Doc yet.

All she hoped was that they weren't going to ruin their chance at a fresh start.

Chapter 12
Doc

August

It was mid-August. The weather had been overcast much of the day—a refreshing break for a warm summer when she'd been working so hard. A light drizzle here and there. Andie had spent much of her time harvesting berries in the tunnels; she was exhausted.

Doc had helped and then offered to whip them up a little breakfast for supper. He'd brought his laptop with him. They sat on her little sofa, cuddled together while she watched the telly and he attempted to write.

Somewhere in the middle of a farming show and Andie arguing with Rupert over treats, Doc found his inspiration. He switched to a new Word document. A new title. A fresh start. He barely noticed when she slowly drifted closer and closer until her head rested against his shoulder.

His typing didn't seem to bother her. Rupert shuffled closer as well. He stretched out across them, so his body was draped across their feet.

It was warm and cosy. Lovely. Doc wished he could bottle up the sensation for himself. To revisit over and over. He didn't quite understand the feeling, but it was beautiful.

His fingers flew across the keys. He barely registered Andie leaning more heavily against him. She mumbled in her sleep, which made him chuckle to himself.

It was magic.

When Doc finally stopped writing, he'd managed two complete chapters. He yawned widely, glancing down to find Andie and Rupert deeply asleep. They had him pinned in with no way to get up without waking either of them.

Saving his document three times, just in case, Doc shut down his laptop and set it to one side. His mind was buzzing with excitement. He had a story; he had words.

Somehow, in the comfort of Andie's home, Doc

had found his creative drive once again. He relaxed back into the cushions, careful not to wake his slumbering companions. He dragged the blanket across all three of them more fully.

His arm slipped around Andie, holding her more securely. Doc didn't think it was a coincidence that words had returned with her. In her home. In the easy comfort they'd almost always had with each other.

He dozed off from one second to the next. No dreams. Just a blissful rest after finally making progress. He woke up long before Andie or Rupert.

His mind was already buzzing with ideas for the next few chapters. Doc grabbed his laptop and immediately began working on his manuscript. A fire had definitely been reignited in his muse.

Time flew by. Doc wasn't even aware of Andie waking up until a hand appeared in front of his face. She snapped her fingers a few times, laughing when he reared back from her in surprise.

"You hungry?"

Doc shook his head, keeping his gaze focused on the screen. He didn't want to lose the thrust of the idea. The words might slip through his fingers like sand, and he couldn't risk that happening again after such a long drought.

"How about coffee or tea? Do you want some caffeine to get you going?"

Doc barely managed a shrug.

"Right. Okay." Andie sat up and shoved the blanket off both of them. She stood beside him, stretching for several minutes in silence. He barely noticed it. "Okay. C'mon, Rups. Why don't we go for a walk? Doc?"

Doc blinked a few times when fingers touched his head. Finally, he glanced up at her. "Yeah?"

"You know what, never mind. I'm just going to back away slowly." Andie walked out of the room, laughing to herself. "Careful, Rups, let's not disturb the process."

Dragging the blanket around his shoulders, Doc situated himself more comfortably. His mind was going almost too fast for his fingers to catch up. He had to slow himself down a number of times when even spellcheck couldn't decipher a typo.

Maybe time to take a breath and slow my mind when even spellcheck goes, "what the bloody hell is that supposed to be?"

He'd managed another chapter when a mug appeared between him and the laptop. "Coffee..."

"I've made a breakfast wrap for both of us. Here. Coffee and sustenance to keep the writing juices flowing." Andie set the plate on the coffee table and handed him the mug. "Someone has to take care of you while you drift on a sea of imagination and prose."

Doc nodded absently. He finally glanced away from his screen when her hand covered his on the mug. "Yes?"

"Figured maybe you wanted to make it all the way to your lips before you tilted the mug?" Andie grinned when he noticed how far from his mouth the cup was. "Want me to hold the wrap for you?"

Doc shoved her hand away but had to laugh at himself. "I may be a little distracted this morning."

"Found your words?" Andie sipped from her own mug.

"I did. Somehow." Doc didn't know how to put into words how at ease he'd felt in her space with her. "I'm afraid they'll vanish on me if I stop for even a second."

"So I take the thesaurus off hold at the bookstore?" Andie teased him while finishing up her wrap. She took one last bite, nudging his leg with her foot when he went back to typing. "At least have some breakfast before disappearing into your imagination again."

"Are you going to need help on the farm?"

"From you? Today? Not a chance. You'd probably walk into every tree in the orchard." Andie grabbed her mug and plate, heading into the kitchen. "I've got a couple helpers coming in this morning to help for a few hours. We've got one last tunnel full of berries to harvest. Then it's time to prepare the orchard."

"How's it been with the helpers?"

"Odd. I have everyone wearing masks, which feels quite like science fiction. We stay six feet apart." Andie shrugged. "I'd rather be overly cautious and keep them all safe than deal with the alternative."

After bullying him into taking a few more sips of coffee and bites of the wrap, Andie left him to his writing. He was surprised she hadn't kicked him out of the cottage. The tiny house was supposed to be his residence at the moment.

But she'd welcomed him.

He didn't have time to dwell on his thoughts and feelings. On the way her care and concern had touched him. Words were itching to get out of his brain.

Another thousand words flew by. Doc forced himself to stand up and stretch. His bladder didn't necessarily appreciate the prolonged delay in moving.

He saved the manuscript several times and then made his way out of the farmhouse. Andie waved from the barn when he passed by. He needed a hot shower and a change of clothes.

His back hadn't appreciated sleeping on a sofa. And it didn't enjoy half a night spent sitting up either. He was getting a little too old for that.

Feeling a little more human after his shower, Doc decided to spend some time outdoors. Words hadn't abandoned him. And being with Andie had seemed to bring them back to him.

"The writer emerges from a deep dark cave. He sees the light for the first time in ages. He lives," Andie called dramatically. She'd moved from the barn and appeared to be stacking boxes onto the trailer attached to the tractor again. "He lives!"

"You are not nearly as amusing as you think." Doc dodged Rupert, who dashed by him, racing after a bumblebee. "How goes the harvest?"

"This is the last of the berries for now." Andie hefted up the last basket. "I staggered my planting so I won't have another polytunnel harvest for a few weeks. It's on to the orchards and a lot of climbing ladders. The brewery is thankfully staying open, or I've no idea what I'd do with barrels of apples."

"A host of pies."

"You are not nearly as amusing as you think." Andie threw his words back at him with a wry chuckle. "Fancy a ride with me down to the end of the lane?"

"In the back of the trailer?"

"We can squish together on the tractor." Andie held her hand out toward him. "Afraid of my driving?"

"I've seen you drive that into a ditch."

"Is that no?" Andie laughed again when he caught her hand.

Doc climbed into the tractor seat, and a second after, Andie situated herself on his lap. "Comfortable?"

"Immensely."

Chapter 13
Andie

September

"What do you think, Rups?" Andie twisted the page around to show Rupert how much of her September to-do list had already been crossed off. "Are we crushing it? Or are we crushing it?"

Her helpers had all gone back to school. Andie had been left with Rupert and her author in residence as back-up on the farm. The September harvest was taking longer than expected but not quite as bad as she'd feared.

Andie pinned the list back onto the board by her bedroom door. "I'm going to miss the end-of-summer pop-up dinner."

For the last few years, Andie had thrown a

supper for her clients in the area, her farmhands, and friends. She didn't think it would happen this year. Not with how there already seemed to be a second wave of the pandemic happening.

She wasn't anxious to take risks for herself or others. What was one year in the grand scheme of things? Maybe if things continued to open up, she might put together a meal and deliver it around the county.

A knock on the door drew her away from her to-do list. Andie followed Rupert through the house to where they found Doc waiting for them. She waved him in, thankful he didn't comment on her pyjamas and bathrobe.

Doc had been spending his days outdoors with her and his evenings writing in her living room. He claimed the words flowed better in her space. She tried not to make any assumptions based on that.

She'd tried to get a preview of his manuscript. He deflected all of her attempts. They'd made a game of it.

It was addicting, having Doc in her home. Around her. All the time. A life she'd ways dreamed about but never thought could come true.

"Morning."

"Is it?" He had the audacity to laugh when she

groaned. "Rough night?"

"Rupert decided he had a desperate need to be outside at four in the morning." Andie dragged her fingers through her hair, attempting to feel a little more presentable. Finally, she slumped into one of the chairs around her little kitchen table. "You'd think, as the boss, I could give myself a day off."

"Don't think farmers get days off."

"Pity. I could use one." Andie went to get up but stopped when Doc moved further into the kitchen. He grabbed her container of coffee and got her kettle going. "Making me coffee?"

"And breakfast. I can't give you a day off, but a few minutes I can manage." Doc began foraging in the fridge. He pulled out several things, deftly moving Rupert out of his way. "You can't have a snack before I've made anything."

"He'll try his best, though." Andie bent forward, folding her arms on the table and resting her head on them. "I don't know why I'm so tired."

"You've been doing the job of four people all summer." Doc broke several eggs into a bowl and whisked them up with a fork. "All of this is stressful and exhausting. Our routines have been thrown to the wind. Everything changes constantly. It's difficult to cope with continuous upheaval and worry, even more so when you're trying to run a family farm in the middle of all of it."

"You're trying to write a book in the middle of it." Andie pointed out. She hadn't really stopped to process what was happening in the world. It was easy to focus instead on keeping up with the harvest. "If I think on it too much, my mind spirals into doom and gloom."

"All I'm saying is maybe we should be kinder to ourselves. Managing to accomplish anything is worthy of celebration." Doc popped a few slices of bread into the toaster. He moved comfortably around her kitchen. "I can manage a good simple omelette."

"More than most people." Andie watched him work for several minutes in silence.

It was nice, more than, actually, to have him so free in her home. They'd been steadily shifting to firmer ground in whatever this new stage of their relationship was. She didn't want to push him.

He'd bolted before.

"Doc?"

"Hmm?" He tossed the dishtowel in his hand over his shoulder and deftly flipped the omelette. "Something wrong?"

"No, I...." Andie wanted to ask if he planned to stay. But she'd mean forever, and it would break her heart to burst her own happy bubble so soon. "Just admiring your technique."

"You're being weirdly neurotypical in a way that I can't decipher." He eyed her few seconds before turning his attention back to the pan. "Have I done something wrong? In your space too much? I can go back to writing in the tiny house. Or outside."

"No, no." Andie held her hands up to stop his rambling. "No. I've loved having you here. Love having you here."

"But?"

"I don't want it to end," she finally admitted.

"Is it going to end?"

"No, it's not," Andie responded a little too quickly.

Doc paused to glance back at her. He shifted the omelette around in the pan. "I don't understand. And I'd like to. What am I missing?"

Rupert offered the briefest distraction by choosing to upend his water dish. Andie cleared up the mess while Doc plated up the omelettes. It gave her time to attempt to bring her thoughts together.

They sat at her old kitchen table. Andie had large mugs of coffee to go with their omelette and toast. She had a few bites; she knew the conversation had to be addressed eventually.

"I'm enjoying you being here. The company. Well, no, not just the company. It's more you than anything," Andie rambled nervously. She scratched Rupert's head absently when he came to lean against her. "I woke up this morning thinking I'd be crushed when you left."

"I'm not leaving. Am I?"

She reminded herself that Doc tended to be quite literal at times. Another bite of omelette offered her a reprieve to think. She didn't want to confuse him; this seemed like a conversation they wanted to get right.

"I suppose...." Andie trailed off. She sipped coffee and started again. "My hope is this is the start of building something together."

"A shed?"

Andie barely managed to avoid snorting coffee out of her nose when she burst out laughing. "A life. A relationship. Us."

"But we did build a shed."

Andie caught the twitch of his lips, turning up into a grin. "We did."

"A nice one."

"It is." She nodded.

"So, maybe this 'us' build will be just as brilliant." Doc grabbed a glass of juice and clinked it against her coffee mug. "Slàinte Mhath."

"Slàinte!" Andie couldn't stop hope from bubbling up inside her again with their light-hearted early morning toast. "Also, less risk of accidentally hammering your thumb with a metaphorical shed."

"Just hammering our hearts." Doc's blue eyes met her brown ones. "Here's to our love shed."

"Oh, you absolute arsehole. I'm going to spend the whole day trying to get a mangled version of that song out of my head." Andie groaned, then lobbed a piece of bacon at him, only for Rupert to snatch it out of the air. "Betrayed by man and beast. I see how it's going to be."

"Is that a no to the love shed?"

Andie dropped her head to the table with a groan. "If I wind up singing that song in the middle of the night, I'm going to... think of something appropriately painful to respond with."

"Buona fortuna."

"Not even half as funny as you think you are." Andie couldn't help grinning when he chuckled. She loved his deep laugh; it reverberated in the kitchen pleasantly. "Going to give me a hand in the orchard?"

"Coffee first. Apples after."

Chapter 14
Doc

October

Leaves had begun to change. Signs of autumn were all around the farm. He could hear geese flying overhead.

The brief reopening of the world had gone about as Doc expected. Premature and ill-advised. The few months had allowed Andie to bring in more help on the farm, but they were back to managing on their own with Rupert's less than helpful but enthusiastic assistance.

Their little bubble on the farm felt safe and cosy. Removed. He knew they were lucky. Privileged to be safe and comfortable in the Scottish countryside.

Andie was throwing herself into projects around

the farm and finishing up the orchard harvest. She worried about her family in Italy. None of them had gotten sick thus far, but it was hard to be so far away from them.

He hoped their luck would continue.

"Knock, knock." Andie poked her head into the open door of his tiny house. "No writing this morning?"

"I sent the first half of my manuscript to my editor last night. Taking a little break to see if I'm on the right track." Doc crouched down to greet Rupert, who'd dashed inside and darted around him. "Morning, young man. Have you chased your tail enough?"

"He's been a right nuisance." Andie leaned against the doorframe and watched them with a smile. "Fancy a walk? It's been so windy. I want to head down to the paddock to check on the new shed and polytunnels."

"Let me grab my coat." Doc pushed himself back up, trying not to groan when his knees popped. He sent a glare at Andie when she laughed at the sound. "Sure you want an old man like me?"

"Too late to back out on me now. I'm attached." Andie was already out the door before he could respond.

Attached.

They hadn't even gone on an actual date. What was a real date anyway? They couldn't go out; neither of them found most societal norms appealing.

It was late in the evening when Doc had a chance to revisit the idea of a date. He spent two hours on Google, searching for anything that might be of interest. Unfortunately, everything he found seemed like something they'd laugh about, not enjoy.

Doc wanted to be comfortable. He was at his best when relaxed. Andie deserved to see him that way.

She deserved to see him at his best. His running had been him at his worst. They needed to be different this time, both of them.

Open, honest, comfortable.

Google failed him. Every date idea was more far-fetched than the last or impossible to manage on a small farm in Aberdeenshire. He steadily grew more frustrated until his phone buzzed with a text from his editor, Essie, offering a much-needed distraction.

Essie: So, how's the farmer?

Doc: Farming.

Essie: Not what I meant.

Doc: I don't know. I don't know how to plan a date with limited supplies and a

lockdown. How do neurotypicals do this shite?

Essie: I'm sending you a package.

Doc: What?

Essie: Do you trust me?

Doc: With my manuscript.

Essie: You both like music and the outdoors, right?

Doc: I'm terrified to say yes.

The box arrived over a week later. Andie and Rupert were both trying to sneak their noses into it. Doc managed to get it into the cottage without their snooping.

Essie had sent him a karaoke machine. A karaoke machine. Doc stared at it for a full minute before bursting out laughing. Maybe it was a good thing the farm was so remote.

The package also contained a plethora of snacks and a case of his favourite Japanese beer. One he'd discovered on his travels and fallen in love with. He wondered where she'd found it.

Cakes, chocolate, crisps, and all sorts of other snacks filled up the space around the beer and karaoke machine. A second box came the following day. She'd gotten groceries delivered to the farm; he shuddered to think about the extra shipping surcharge.

In the second box, Essie had put together all the ingredients required to make his favourite version of ramen, a bit of a hodgepodge of a few recipes that he'd found while avoiding writing. Doc was always amazed at what other things he accomplished while not putting pen to paper.

After all the farming chores were accomplished, it was late in the day when Doc set the first surprise down on her coffee table. Andie stared at it. Rupert chose to sniff every inch of the box he could reach.

"Karaoke."

"Yes." Doc wasn't sure if her stunned amazement was excited or horrified in nature. "Karaoke."

"Brilliant." She trailed her fingers across the top of the box. "I'll have to get Rupert earmuffs. He might not appreciate our caterwauling."

"Or he might join in."

Leaving Andie inspecting the machine, Doc carried the rest of what he'd brought into the kitchen. He set the box of snacks to one side and began organizing the ramen ingredients. Essie had included the curly wheat noodles he preferred along with a good bone broth.

He had all the spices and sauces required to

make his favourite glazed chicken and shiitake mushroom ramen. Essie had included the latter but correctly assumed they'd have most of the vegetables he'd need. His mouth was already watering while getting everything prepared.

Rolling up his sleeves, Doc dug around in one of the cabinets to find a cutting board. He grabbed a knife. Cooking kept his nerves from getting the best of him; it had been a clever idea from Essie.

Put him in his comfort zone, and maybe he wouldn't make a fool of himself.

"What's all this?" Andie joined him in the kitchen. She motioned to the cabinet next to the fridge when he asked about a pot. "Doc?"

"Our first 'real' date." Doc diced up some garlic. He preferred to have all the ingredients ready before he started to cook. "Ramen, beer, and a song for our supper."

"Our first...." Andie's gaze darted from him to his mise en place, then down at her dusty dungarees. "I'll be right back."

Mixing up the marinade for the chicken, Doc spared a glance at Rupert, who didn't appear to know what had happened either. Andie had vanished on them. Then, a few seconds later, they heard the water going.

Rupert sat beside him and pawed at his leg.

"I've no idea what's going on with her either. The inner workings of Andie's mind are beyond me." Doc chuckled when Rupert nudged him again. "Wanting a treat, are we? You'll have to be patient. Not sure you want to eat a load of garlic. It certainly won't improve your breath."

Ruper seemed to frown up at him. Doc wasn't sure if it was the comment on his breath, the lack of treat, or his own imagination. He laughed at himself and returned to working on dinner.

A first date hadn't seemed an overly stressful idea until Andie had dashed off. Doc hoped he hadn't been reading the signs wrong. He didn't think he had.

Was I supposed to do something special? Should I have specifically said this was a first date in advance? Bugger. I should've. There are probably rules for this.

"Well, it's too late to fix it now." Doc scrounged around in the cupboard to find the box of Rupert's treats. He tossed one over to him. "Keep your paws crossed for me, Rupert. We're in uncharted territory."

Chapter 15
Andie

October

A FIRST DATE.

A real first date.

It was a date. Andie couldn't wear muddy dungarees and a T-shirt. It had been a long day on the farm; she'd been dealing with another clogged irrigation system in her newest polytunnel. A grimy, muddy, soggy day. She'd intended to dive into clean pyjamas and spend her evening watching trashy shows on the telly.

A first date wasn't pyjamas in front of the telly. Tossing her dungarees into the laundry basket in the bathroom, Andie took the quickest shower of her life. She was starving and excited about their evening.

It felt a little silly. They'd spent almost every evening together for the past however many months since the pandemic began. But this seemed different.

A first.

A fresh start to the debacle of their first kiss.

Andie didn't quite know what to wear. Doc had on a pair of jeans and a long-sleeved shirt. *I will not be ridiculous. I will be myself—not a fancy version.*

He likes me.

Oh.

He does actually like me, and we're having a real date.

Calming herself down, Andie sorted through her clothes. Finally, she settled on a comfy non-muddy pair of jeans and a Rolling Stones T-shirt. Cleaner than dirty dungarees while allowing her to relax and be comfortable to enjoy the evening.

And the ramen.

Her stomach loudly protested the delay in having supper. Andie pulled on a pair of socks. The floor was definitely too cold to be wandering around barefoot.

Rupert skittered down the hall toward her when the bedroom door opened. He squirmed around and then darted back to the kitchen. Andie followed at a calmer pace; she stopped to stoke the fire.

The weather had already turned colder, and the wind had been fierce the last day or so. Andie kept the fire going through the night to avoid freezing in the cottage. She returned to the kitchen to find Rupert sitting by Doc's feet, begging for a treat.

"Nice timing." Doc had two bowls on the counter. He was using chopsticks to arrange the sliced chicken on top of the noodles. She leaned against the counter and snagged one of the slices on the chopping board. He swatted her knuckles. "Thief."

"It's for eating, right?" Andie licked off the sauce the chopsticks had left on her knuckles. "How much has Rupert conned out of you?"

"I'll never tell."

They both laughed when Rupert rolled over on his back. Andie grabbed one of the bowls for herself. They got comfortable in the living room to eat.

"Rups. Behave yourself." Andie waited until Rupert went to stretch out in front of the fire before settling down with her ramen. "How'd you get all of this delivered?"

"You'll have to ask my editor. She's secretly a wizard." Doc was far more adept at using chopsticks than Andie. She stuck with her fork and spoon to slurp up the noodles. "I discovered the limits of Google."

"Oh?"

"Date ideas that don't make me want to fall on my pen."

"Fall on your pen?"

"Less painful and permanently harmful than falling on a sword." Doc used his chopsticks to toss a bite of chicken at Rupert. "And I currently lack a sword."

"Hopefully, not the only thing preventing you from falling on one." Andie grinned before taking a massive bite of ramen. "What's the worst idea you saw?"

"Pottery classes."

"Pottery classes?"

"I am not Patrick Swayze," Doc grumbled when she poked him in the side. "All that clay under my fingers? No, thank you. Writing is my one and only creative endeavour. I craft words into art—no mess or pottery wheels required."

It was cosy and warm, sitting on the couch and joking together. Their empty bowls rested on the coffee table. Andie had shifted over to lean against Doc's side while Rupert had drifted off in front of the fire.

"What's your go-to karaoke song?" Andie broke the silence after allowing the fog of food to start to clear. "Mine has to be from Queen."

"Any particular one, or 'God Save...'?" Doc trailed off when she burst out laughing.

"Not nearly as funny as you think you are."

"Yet you laughed." Doc stopped fidgeting with his chopsticks when she placed her hand over his. "Probably something by the Stones."

They were delaying the inevitable. Doc had set up the karaoke machine. They'd gotten it plugged in —tested some of the music available via streaming.

"I can't." Andie covered her face with one hand while clutching the mic in her other. She listened while the bars of a song by Queen played. "This is much easier when I'm in the shower singing into my shampoo bottle."

"Want me to get your shampoo for you?" Doc offered without even the hint of a smile.

From anyone else, Andie would know they were poking fun at her. Doc had been serious, though. His unique approach to life often surprised her.

"I'll manage. Let me restart."

Two songs and the rest of the six-pack of beer later, the nerves had vanished entirely. Andie was setting up the next tune while Doc belted out a Billy

Joel hit. They'd laughed so much that her sides already ached.

Rupert was slumped at her feet. He wagged his tail and peered pitifully up at her. She bent down to rub his head.

"Poor Rups." She chuckled when he whined mournfully. "Have we worn out your eardrums? Are you wanting your last evening walk?"

"Why don't we take him out? Wind's died down a bit." Doc immediately turned off the mic. He reached over to pause the music. "I'm suddenly glad you don't have any neighbours closer."

"Not sure the cats appreciated our attempts at a serenade." Andie grabbed the set of wellies she kept by the cottage's back door and threw on one of her coats. "Come on, Rups. Out into the cold with us."

It was a beautiful moonlit evening. Rupert dashed about, chasing shadows only he could see. Andie stood beside Doc, leaning into him when he hesitantly looped an arm around her shoulders.

"Is there a date version of a staycation?"

"Staycation," Doc repeated the word with a high level of disgust in his voice. "My least favourite made-up word."

"It's in the dictionary." Andie loved how

pedantic he sometimes got. "All words could be considered made-up ones."

"And this date was going so well." Doc kept his gaze on Rupert.

She didn't take it personally, since eye contact tended to make him uncomfortable. She wanted him to feel at ease with her. "Best date I've had."

"Ever?"

"We can probably improve on it." Andie peered up at him. "Is it a no touch sort of day?"

"It's a one kiss sort of day." Doc twisted toward her. He brought his hand up to cup the side of her face. His gaze focused on her lips while he bent down to brush his against them. "Just the one."

Chapter 16
Doc

November

Time seemed to simultaneously fly by yet drag on. They'd resigned themselves to being isolated at the farm through the rest of the year. Doc knew they were lucky to be together.

Lucky to have a safe, quiet place amid the chaos.

His words had continued to flow. Both his agent and editor were thrilled. Finally, they had hope for hitting his deadline.

Any deadline.

The tenth deadline he'd been given on this particular work-in-progress. They were kind enough not to remind him. The red lines on his calendar going back through the past year or more taunted him often enough to make up for it.

"Doc?"

"Under the tree." Doc didn't glance up from where he was typing away.

"I have a million trees on the farm." Andie's voice came from somewhere behind him.

"The large one." Doc tuned her out again while trying to wrap up the last paragraph. Rupert found him first, flopping across his lap and dislodging his laptop. "Are you going to be my beta reader?"

"Are you waiting for an apple to drop on your head?" Andie strolled between the trees toward him. "How goes the writing?"

"Added a few more chapters." Doc saved his novel several times, just to make sure, then closed his computer. "My editor should be pleased, terrible taskmaster that she is."

"Rups. Doc doesn't need a writing assistant." Andie tried to pull Rupert away from Doc, but he flopped over on his back instead. He huffed excitedly when Doc rubbed his belly. "Spoiled mutt."

After a few seconds of entertaining Rupert, Doc got to his feet. He put his laptop under his arm. Andie whistled for her dog, who finally listened and went over to her side.

"Fancy lunch? I've gathered up some salad ingredients from one of the greenhouses." Andie took a tennis ball out of her pocket and sent Rupert flying after it. "It's surprisingly mild and sunny for November."

"Lunch and a walk?"

"Maybe not at the same time." Doc quickly fell in step with her while they made their way through the orchard. He'd enjoyed writing amongst the trees. "Your orchard made for quite the inspiring spot today."

They picked their way through the orchard in silence. Andie stopped when they reached the edge. She slipped her arm around his.

Most of the leaves were gone from the trees. A few brightly autumn-coloured ones held out here and there. He had a feeling they might be in for a cold and blustery winter.

"We'll spend Christmas alone this year, I think." Andie sounded sad, though he wasn't entirely sure. "I don't mind being alone with you. I'm enjoying it."

"But?"

"It's the holidays."

"I'm sorry you're going to miss your family." Doc had learned the hard way that practical thoughts weren't helpful when dealing with emotional subjects. "Is it hard? Not seeing all the people you usually do?"

"A little." Andie looped her arm around his while they strolled up the lane toward the cottage. "Do you miss people?"

"Maybe?" Doc shrugged. He had Andie and Rupert. Everyone else in his life was easily reached via text message or email. It didn't strike him the same way it seemed to do her. "It's an abstract thing for me."

"Abstract?"

"Missing people." Doc had a wealth of emotions in him, but they didn't always make sense. "In the abstract. They're still there. I talk to them—mostly via email."

"Out of sight, out of mind?"

"Not exactly. I care about my friends and family. Deeply. But I'm not always as connected as everyone else seems." Doc had struggled with it in his twenties, trying to meet everyone else's expectations. Family connections had always been a little difficult for him to deal with. "Maintaining relationships is sometimes beyond the scope of my capabilities."

"You read that somewhere." Andie smiled, likely to show she was teasing him.

"Maybe the wording." Doc had a tendency to

inhale the things he read, practically imprinting phrases on his mind if they struck his fancy. "I do my best."

"Your best is brilliant and enough."

"Not for everyone." Doc didn't have a smile in him. He'd lost friends over the years because of his difficulties. One of the most potent things Doc had learned was sometimes people weren't meant to be in your life. "But then again, maybe I'm just not for everyone."

"It's a good thing I'm not everyone." Andie patted his arm. "No one should be forced to meet some sort of shite expectations."

They were silent for a bit. Doc thought maybe he could do something for the holidays. Andie obviously cared about them a great deal; there was no getting around this year would be very different.

"I enjoy the quiet and joy others experience during the holidays." He wondered how he might make December memorable for Andie. Little things, big ones. What could he manage while stuck in the middle of Aberdeenshire? "We might still find some Christmas magic for you this year."

"Maybe."

While Andie sorted together lunch, Doc considered his options. Essie had done wonders with helping on their first date. He fished his phone out of his pocket and sent a quick text to her; she immediately agreed to help him think of some options.

"Deep in thought." Andie tossed a bit of cucumber at his head. Then, she went back to whisking up a dressing for their salads, a mixture of olive oil, sweet balsamic vinegar, and macerated berries that she'd smashed up along with some fresh herbs from her garden. "New idea for your story?"

"Just sharing a thought with Essie, my editor. She's a godsend." Doc knew he'd gotten lucky with his editor and agent. They'd both gone out of their way to meet him where he was. He knew they did a lot of extra work to accommodate his needs. Other autistic authors in his writing group weren't so lucky. "She's brilliant."

"Of course she is; she works with you." Andie continued whisking up the dressing. "Give me a hand with dicing up some of these little tomatoes?"

"Maybe I'm brilliant because of the people I surround myself with." He nudged her gently with his elbow. "Yourself included."

"Well, I think you don't give yourself enough credit." Andie added another dash of vinegar to the dressing. "Is it difficult to deal with the publishing world?"

"In general? Or as an autistic?"

Andie considered for a moment before answering him. "Both."

"Not sure I can speak for non-autistic authors. I'd say it's more complicated than it needs to be at times." Doc grabbed another handful of cherry tomatoes and began slicing them up. "Most advice out there is written for them—not autistics."

"That doesn't seem fair."

"Maybe." Doc shrugged. "I've been quite lucky with the people around me. They go out of their way to help me bridge the gaps whenever necessary. Not sure I'm talented enough to deserve it."

"You don't have to be talented to deserve a world that's accessible to you, Doc." Andie pointed her whisk at him, ignoring the dressing dripping from it. "Besides, I believe I've already mentioned you're brilliant."

"Yes, well."

"There's nothing wrong with needing a hand in making the world an even playing field. That's what accessibility is." Andie gestured with the whisk before returning to the dressing. "Just making things equal."

Chapter 17
Andie

December

IT STARTED THE FIRST MORNING OF DECEMBER. Crisp, frosty air outside. Andie found an excited Rupert dancing around by the door. She let him out and then followed, stepping out into a bizarre, wonderful new world.

Normally on December mornings, or any winter day, really, Andie went out into the bitter cold darkness. It was generally hours before the sun came up. Today bright lights twinkled everywhere around her and in the distance, as though she'd stepped into the stars.

It was magical. Crisp wintery frost with

sparkling fairy lights. As though snowflakes had come to life around her.

Strings of lights framed her cottage and the barn in the distance. Little lamps lined the paths around the farm. She thought there might have been lamps dangling from trees in the orchard, but it was hard to tell.

"What on earth is happening? Did you sneak out, Rups?" Andie laughed when he pranced around her and then dashed off down the path. "Add a little twinkle to our farm?"

There were no other decorations. Just strings of lights and little lanterns. Andie immediately went to the small cottage. She knocked on the door when she noticed the lights on inside.

Doc opened the door a sliver and peered out at her. "Morning."

"You going to let us in?" Andie grinned at him.

"No." Doc closed the door on her.

Andie stared at the door for a full five seconds, then glanced down at Rupert, who wagged his tail. "Odd things are afoot, Rups."

On the second day of December, Andie woke up to find three wreaths around the farm. One on the cottage and one on the tiny house, along with a third on the barn doors. They were beautifully simple and suited her style, with plaid ribbon intricately woven with evergreen foliage, dried oranges, and pinecones.

The following morning, Andie found a little tray of breakfast tartlets and a coffee thermos on her kitchen counter. They were squares of puff pastry filled with bacon, sausage, and a perfectly fried egg in the centre. She frowned down at Rupert, who was trying to sneak one off the table.

"You're a terrible guard dog, Rups." Andie munched on one of the pastries while wandering around the kitchen, making herself a cup of coffee. "How about we take some of this over to see if we can get a sneak at what Doc's hiding in the cottage, eh?"

No amount of cajoling could convince Doc to allow her inside. He slipped outside, shutting the door behind him. His attempt at an air of innocence was only mildly better than Rupert's when he'd snuck a sausage off her plate at breakfast.

Every single day brought a fresh surprise. On the seventh, Andie awoke to a fully decorated tree in her living room and the smell of food being cooked. She hadn't heard a thing.

How was he doing it?

Doc was in her kitchen, casually cooking breakfast like nothing had changed. "Morning."

"Have you by any chance been sneaking sleeping pills in snacks for Rupert?" Andie stared in awe at the tree while Doc continued mucking about in the kitchen. "How is he not waking up.?"

There was a pause.

"I am joking," Andie clarified. "You're sneaky."

Doc nodded and returned his attention to whatever he was fixing up for breakfast. "All the magic of Santa."

"Santa?"

"Long beard, red suit, creepy bastard who sneaks into your house without being invited." Doc eyed her thoughtfully for a second before they both burst out laughing. "Ever consider how truly terrifying some childhood fables are when seen through the lens of adulthood?"

"They weren't meant for adults—but yes."

"I once argued with my parents that anyone who barters for teeth while I'm sleeping should be reported to the police." Doc motioned for her to join him in the kitchen. He nodded to the mugs of coffee already prepared. "I refused to put even one under my pillow."

"The tooth fairy? You argued about getting free money?"

"Money for teeth. My teeth. Am I the only person to find it odd?" Doc shuddered.

Something about the image of wee Docherty Fabre debating the disturbing nature of the tooth fairy at five years old sent her into uncontrollable giggles. Andie grabbed onto the counter and tried to stop laughing. He sighed, waiting for her to finish.

"I can't...." Andie trailed off into another fit of snickering. She held her sides. "Oh, it hurts. I can't breathe."

"You're talking."

Andie fell back on everything she'd learned as a mature adult and stuck her tongue out at him. "Are you planning on doing something every morning?"

"A magician never gives away his secrets."

No matter how Andie tried. Doc refused to provide any further answers. She found herself trying to guess what might come next.

Every morning had brought some surprise, whether large or small. It was the most amazing advent calendar to have ever been gifted. Andie fell a little more in love with him each day.

Despite all her best efforts, she hadn't been able to discover what he'd planned for Christmas Eve. She had a lot of her own traditions for the day. But without her family, they all seemed pointless.

Andie went to sleep the day before with a slightly dimmed mood.

She missed her family. For the first time since the start of pandemic, she wasn't able to simply push aside those thoughts. There was no getting around their absence during the holidays.

"We'll manage, right, Rups?" Andie wrapped her arms around him and tried to find a silver lining. "At least we're all healthy and safe."

Christmas Eve dawned bright and early; Andie had woken up to no surprise at all. She wasn't quite sure how to react. Maybe things had finally come to an end.

All the decorations were up across the farm and in the cottage. There had been so many little treats, from holiday-themed pyjamas to scented bath bombs. She felt well and truly spoiled by him.

It was late in the evening when Rupert repeatedly barked by the back door. Andie threw her thick bathrobe over her pyjamas and shoved her feet into her boots. Her dog's bladder waited for no one.

"Come on then, Rups. One last time before bed." Andie frowned when she heard voices. She made her way toward the back of the barn. "What the—"

Doc had somehow strung a sheet up across the back of the barn. He had a projector playing one of her favourite holiday films. Two lounge chairs with several blankets sat on either side of a portable steel container where a roaring fire was going. "Merry Christmas Eve."

"Doc."

"You've got a tradition with your parents to watch *A Christmas Carol* every twenty-fourth." Doc grabbed a tablet she hadn't noticed. He twisted it around to show her parents on Zoom. "I thought you three might enjoy it this way. You can prop them up and...."

"Doc." Andie found herself in tears at his thoughtfulness. She'd been missing her parents. Ignoring them on Zoom for a moment, she rushed over to throw her arms around him. "Thank you."

"Those are happy tears, right? I can never tell."

"Whatever you do, don't kiss in front of us. I have innocent eyes." Her father's teasing voice came out from the tablet in Doc's hand. "Very innocent eyes."

"It's the only part of him that's innocent." Her grandmother spoke up from off-screen.

"Nonna." Andie backed away from Doc, offering him a slight apology before taking the tablet. "Buon Natale."

They all greeted her. She laughed a little teary-eyed when her grandparents squeezed into frame behind her parents. They were all there.

Healthy and there.

Andie didn't think she could ask for anything more for the holidays, particularly this year. She grabbed Doc's hand when he went to walk away. "Watch with us?"

"You sure?"

Andie squeezed his hand gently. She wanted him to feel like part of the family. They'd been inching closer and closer to that over the course of the last year. "It wouldn't be the same without you."

"Were we ever this nauseating?" Her father broke into the conversation again.

"Constantly," her nonna retorted immediately. "Worse."

Chapter 18
Doc

December

Christmas morning came early. Doc had one more surprise up his sleeve, but he hadn't anticipated how much energy planning and executing everything would require. He was tired.

While Doc had zero regrets over making December memorable for Andie, he'd pushed himself a little too far. A meltdown or shutdown seemed almost inevitable. He'd been neglecting the measures he usually took to relax and help calm his mind.

He knew better. There was a lifetime of experience in dealing with sensory overload and being overwhelmed. But sometimes, it was hard not to push himself.

And he had.

Staying in bed was an attractive idea. Doc counted all the lines on the duvet, starting over when he lost track. His brain felt heavy. He reached blindly for his earbuds and phone, putting them in and finding his favourite music playlist—a mixture of classic rock.

Three songs into the playlist, Doc found his shoulders lowering. His breathing evened out. The heaviness lightened enough for him to climb out of bed.

Changing out of his plaid pyjamas required far too much effort. Doc stayed as he was. He'd intended to sneak into the main cottage for one last surprise. A glance at his watch told him he was probably too late.

"Doc?" Andie knocked lightly on the door. "You all right? I've made a batch of cornetto alla marmellata. Used the berry jam my friend made. A special little Italian breakfast treat for us."

Words weren't coming to him. Instead, Doc dragged himself over to the door. He slowly opened it, staring down at Rupert to avoid Andie's gaze; eye contact was always hard, but impossible on days like this.

"Ah." Andie immediately lowered her voice to almost a whisper. "Having a no-word duvet day?"

Doc nodded. He brushed his fingers through Rupert's fur, an infinitely soothing feeling. The Airedale pressed himself against his leg.

"You've made my December the best I've ever had. Why don't I return the favour?" Andie placed a hand on his arm briefly. "I'll leave Rupert to keep you company. I'll bring you a breakfast tray. I've got loads of chores around the farm. And if you're up for it, later we can have lunch or supper together. Whatever you need."

He nodded again. It was like trying to pull words through a fog. A thick fog made out of treacle. And it was more than he could currently manage.

"Right. You get cosy. I'll bring food," Andie promised.

She was gone in a swirl of her thick robe and the strand of tinsel around her neck. Doc expected Rupert to chase after her, but the dog seemed content to sit by his side, as if he sensed the shift in his mood.

Sinking into one of the beanbag chairs in the tiny living room, Doc reclined. He smiled when Rupert rested his chin on his leg. The dog huffed until he went back to petting him.

The silence in the room was too heavy for him. Doc needed more white noise. Something to block out the sound of the ticking clock, of Rupert's snuffling, of all the little things that other people might overlook but were like a jet engine for him. He grabbed his laptop and queued up a holiday-themed YouTube video with instrumental music and a crackling fire in the background.

Andie returned after a while. He'd spent the whole time petting Rupert and relaxing, allowing the music to wash over him. "I've brought several of these jam-filled pastries I made and some coffee."

She set the large platter and two mugs on the little table between the beanbags. He was surprised when she made herself comfortable in the other seat. He'd assumed she'd return to the cottage.

Doc grabbed the coffee and peered at her over the rim of the mug.

"We don't have to natter. There's music. Fairy lights overhead. And cornetti." Andie kept her voice low, which was a relief. "Just share our Christmas breakfast in companionable silence."

Doc nodded.

"Buon Natale." Andie grabbed one of the pastries.

Doc took a bite of his own. It was dense and

sweet, like the love child of a croissant and brioche. The jam made a perfect burst of flavour.

Despite the rough start to his day, Andie, as always, had found a way to vastly improve it for him. He inhaled two of the pastries. Rupert shifted even closer to him, staring mournfully up at him while he took his last bite.

When the pastries were gone and the mugs empty, Andie pulled a package out of her pocket. She tossed it into his lap. Doc inspected the present while she gathered up the empty cups and plate.

"Come on, Rups. Time to walk the farm." She started toward the door, stopping when Doc got to his feet. "Everything okay? I figured I'd check in on you around lunchtime—see if you're up to joining me."

Doc set his unopened package on the table. "I can walk."

"We should both probably put something other than pyjamas on." Andie glanced down at her thick robe, then over at him. "Meet outside in a few minutes?"

"Okay."

The fresh air would be good for him, probably. Doc quickly swapped his pyjamas for something more winter-appropriate. He wasn't surprised when an enthusiastic Rupert dashed between the tiny cottage and where Andie already waited for him.

"Calm yourself, Rupert. I'm here." He laughed when Rupert leapt up at him. "Easy there. Can we skip the muddy paws just this once?"

"Rups." Andie shook her head and whistled for her dog. "Sorry. I swear he's in rare form this morning. He's always excited when he opens his stocking."

"His stocking?"

"Of course. I fill it with treats. He's had the same one since he was a puppy." Andie pulled a new tennis ball out of her pocket and sent it flying down the path. "Feeling better?"

"Mildly." Doc found the muffled sensation in his ears had lessened. It no longer felt like his entire head had been stuffed with cotton balls. "Mostly."

They meandered through several of the polytunnels. Doc played fetch with Rupert while Andie checked on the irrigation systems. A daily task. He knew she'd lost a quarter of her harvest once because of broken equipment; he didn't blame her for inspecting them more frequently.

"I'd planned one last surprise for you today." Doc had wanted to finish the holiday surprise on the twenty-five. Unfortunately, he didn't have the energy for it. "Sorry."

"For what? Making the entire month of December magical for me? It made missing my family a lot less painful." Andie dusted her hands off on her dungarees. She bent down to grab the ball when Rupert spat it out at her feet. "Thanks, Rups."

The Airedale raced on ahead of them toward the orchard. Doc hoped he hadn't ruined her morning. He'd wanted it to be special.

It mattered a great deal to him. More than he'd expected. Somehow, in the middle of their second chance, he'd fallen further in love than he'd imagined possible.

What if she didn't feel as deeply as he did?

What if Andie wanted him to leave the farm?

"Doc? You all right?" She caught him by the arm. "You look like you've seen a ghost."

"No. I'm not suddenly clairvoyant." Doc waved off her concern. "Maybe the ghost of Christmas past."

"You sure?"

Not a ghost.

Maybe an apparition of future heartache.

They made their loop around the farm in companionable silence. Rupert darted off on adventures before looping back to them every so often. Doc thought he wanted to make sure they didn't disappear on him.

When they made their way back, Andie told him to bring his unopened present up to the cottage. She'd made her nonna's mulled wine and had a selection of cookies that her family had sent. He decided to let go of his plans for the day.

He'd spent twenty-four days making plans. It wasn't the end of the world to miss out on the last one. Besides, Andie seemed to have ideas of her own.

"Doc?"

"Hmm?"

Andie grabbed his hand. She waited for a second as if giving him time to pull away. "You've made this the best Christmas just by being here. No grander gestures required."

Doc shrugged.

Their walk took up a fair bit of the morning. Doc found himself breathing easier. His shoulders had finally relaxed down from being bunched up practically to his ears; he didn't feel like guitar strings that had been too tightly wound anymore.

Laughter returned when Rupert dodged and weaved around them, leading Andie on a merry chase through one of the open paddocks. Doc leaned against the fence to watch. It occurred to him that the farm—and Andie—had become home in the past year.

Home.

He'd never been attached to a place, not really. This was different. He couldn't imagine leaving once the world opened up once again.

How could he think about leaving home?

"I'm going to begin fixing up our Christmas lunch. We're going all Italian this year." Andie tossed Rupert's tennis ball in the direction of the farm. "You're welcome to relax in the tiny cottage or come sit while I cook."

"I could help."

Andie smiled brightly at him. "Excellent. I'll pour the wine."

Following her into the cottage, Doc could see she'd already been working hard. There was a platter of cookies off to one side. He could see a bowl with a towel over it with some sort of bread dough.

"What are we having?"

"Lasagne." Andie pulled a dish out of the fridge. "It's ready to pop in the oven. We've got bread, lasagne, lamb chops, salad, and your personal favourite—sticky toffee pudding."

"How can I help?" Doc leaned against the

kitchen counter, accepting the glass of wine from her. "Dicing up the veggies?"

Turning up the music, Andie grabbed her bread. She punched down the dough and got it ready for another rest period. Doc grabbed the colander of veggies fresh from the greenhouse. He rinsed them and simply enjoyed spending time in the kitchen with her.

Time flew by while they prepared a meal. Andie got her family on Zoom for a few minutes. Doc stayed in the background, allowing them to be loud and enthusiastic with each other.

It was sweet to watch but a little overwhelming to listen to. Doc focused on slicing up the veggies for salad. Andie had already made the vinaigrette to go with it.

"They're loud," Andie commented when she finally ended the Zoom call.

"Scottish and Italian blood wasn't going to make for wallflowers." Doc saluted her with his wineglass before taking a sip. "I'm glad you were able to spend time with those you love. That's what the holidays are for."

"Then it's a good thing you're here." Andie had made a nest of blankets on the sofa. She'd already gotten the fireplace going. "Why don't we fix plates and get cosy by the fire? I can put music on or a movie."

They wound up cuddling together on her sofa before a roaring fire, under a large handmade quilt from her nonna. Doc rarely fully relaxed in someone else's company as he did with Andie.

"I love you."

"What?" Doc opened his eyes. He'd been dozing off in the cosy warmth.

"I do love you." Andie stretched an arm out to grab one of the pizzelle off the plate on the coffee table. "I have for years, even if I never dared to say the words. I love you—and I'm hoping you feel the same."

Doc thought about a million different quotes on love. He even had a sonnet or two memorised from his university days. None of them seemed adequate to express his emotions. "I love you."

There was a silence filled only with the munching of cookies. Andie adjusted the quilt over them both. Finally, she offered him a chunk of her pizzella.

"Feels inadequate," Doc commented after a while. "I love you. Too simple. Too few words. Not enough to encompass all of the emotions encapsulated in my very being."

"Writing me a sonnet?"

"Halfway to a sonnet." Doc smiled when she rested her head against his shoulder. "Merry Christmas, Andriana."

"Buon natale, Docherty."

Chapter 19
Andie

January

"I'm what?" Andie dragged her spare pillow over her head and groaned loudly into it. "A sea of lucid dreams? I'm far too sober and uncaffeinated to figure out what it means. Rups? Do you think I can get hazard pay for the trauma Nonna put on me with her meditation app?"

Rupert leapt onto the bed and flopped across her. Andie burst out laughing when he dragged the pillow off her face. He definitely wasn't fazed by her dreaming about the now-deleted app.

Sitting up in bed, Andie tossed her pillow to the side and gently nudged Rupert further down. He wagged his tail excitedly. She grabbed her phone and turned off the alarm that had woken her up.

"What's on the to-do list today?" Andie pulled up the app where she jotted down notes each night for her plans for the next day. "Ah. Time to start clearing out the beds in the first four polytunnels. And talk to Doc about moving into the farmhouse and changing the tiny cottage into his writing studio."

She had no idea how Doc would react. He might panic. She hoped he didn't; communication was definitely going to be critical.

After letting Rupert out for his morning run, Andie got coffee and toast. She was a little anxious to start the conversation with Doc. Her mind kept going over all the ways it could go wrong.

She had most of the morning to consider. Doc had been ensconced in front of his laptop, working on edits, when she'd popped by the tiny cottage to leave coffee and breakfast for him. It was hours before he came out to find her.

"Do you want to live with me?" Andie blurted while clearing out her tenth raised planting bed of the day. She was elbow-deep in dirt and muck. "Doc?"

"We already live together." Doc latched onto that particular point. "On the same farm."

Andie dragged her fingers through her hair a few times, regretting it immediately when she realized how much dirt covered her hands. She didn't want to get frustrated when they were obviously having some sort of miscommunication. Doc was rarely pedantic for the sake of being a stubborn git. "Not in the same cottage."

"Takes like five seconds to get from one to the other. Okay." Doc held his hands up when she gave a huff of frustration. "It feels like we're saying the same thing, but we're obviously not. Maybe different words? More words? Something?"

"You love me."

"Yes." Doc nodded.

"I love you." Andie waited until he nodded for a second time before continuing. "And we like cuddling together."

"Why are you stating the obvious?"

"We're snugglers. Kissers. And we're in love. So..."

"You want to live together?"

"I'm explaining this badly," Andie sighed.

"Or I'm understanding badly." Doc moved closer

to her. He reached out to take her hands where she was fidgeting. "Tell me."

"People who love each other live together." Andie had definitely not practised this conversation in her head enough, and she was running out of words. "Don't they?"

"Just tell me. I'll muddle my way through figuring it out." Doc had apparently grasped it was important, whatever she wanted to tell him. "Andie?"

"Not overly interested in weddings, dresses, rings, and crying like a numpty in front of a crowd of people we never see most of the time. I do want to spend my life with you." Andie got it all out in one breath. Then, she focused her attention on Rupert, who had come up to squeeze between them. "In the same cottage."

"As a couple?"

"As a couple," she repeated.

"Officially, but not matrimonially." Doc laughed when Rupert finally succeeded in pressing his body in the small space between them. His wagging tail bashed against both of their legs. "Easy there, Rups."

"Officially as a couple." She had to chuckle with him. "We're talking in circles."

"You dig in the mud. I'll write some words. We'll

circle back to the conversation later." Doc leaned over Rupert and squeezed her into his arms. He pressed a kiss to the top of her head. "I'm not going to leave you standing in the orchard again. I promise."

"Okay." Andie didn't get a chance to say anything else since he gave her one last squeeze and then strode out of the polytunnel. She smiled when Rupert darted toward the exit and back to her. "Go on. Keep him company if you want."

With a rueful chuckle and shake of her head, Andie returned to the next raised bed. She'd made decent progress in clearing out the last harvest's remnants. This was her least favourite part of running the farm.

By noon, Andie managed to clear out the rest of the polytunnel. She'd gotten all of them prepped for the new seedlings. Planting would start in a few weeks if the shipment ever arrived.

Her shipment of new berry seedlings was a few weeks late. The pandemic had slowed everything down. Andie counted herself lucky to be getting them at all, given the current state of affairs.

The impending snow likely wouldn't help matters. They often got a little snow in winter. But a storm was brewing according to the weather forecast;

she planned to spend the rest of the afternoon making sure everything was ready.

They might get a dusting of snow, or a gale might blow up on them and bury them in snow. Andie preferred to prepare for the latter and be pleasantly surprised by the former. She'd already stocked up on food supplies and gotten wood for the fireplace—if the power went out.

Lunch was a quiet affair. Andie made a sandwich with leftovers and sat by the fire with Rupert. Doc had yet to make an appearance.

The wind picked up by the time they stepped back outside. It had turned bitterly cold. They were definitely in for a rough few days.

"Once more into the breach?" Andie laughed when Rupert pressed against her side instead of racing off ahead of her. She scratched his head. "Why don't we check on the barn first? Make sure all the cats are fed and water—and warm enough."

Rupert poked his head out into the blustery wind. Andie followed him outside. She had to carefully close the door to keep from getting it ripped out of her hand.

"Hello, darlings. How are we doing? All warm and snuggly?" Andie double-checked their food and water. She also ensured everything was secured in and around the barn. "Well, Rups? Let's take a quick walk around all the polytunnels and ensure nothing's flying away."

The snow started halfway through her trek around the farm. She found a couple loose ties on one of the new tunnels. It took forever to get them fixed.

She was cold.

Too cold.

Everything took longer while her fingers struggled to cope. Rupert whined anxiously at her side. She managed to get the last tie back into place, but she'd begun to shiver uncontrollably.

"Let's get back to the cottage, Rups." Andie tried to get her gloves back on, but she kept dropping them. "*Bugger.*"

Chapter 20
Doc

January

"Andie?" Doc kicked the snow off his boots before stepping into the cottage and shutting the door behind him. He winced at the high-pitched howling wind outside. "Andie? Why's it so cold in here?"

Rupert whined from the living room. Doc found himself shivering despite his coat. He followed the sound to find Andie under a blanket with her dog on top of her.

"What the—" Doc quickly jerked off his coat. He rushed over to get the fire going, stoking the embers. He put the kettle on, turned the temperature on the radiators up and then returned to the sofa. "Andie? How long were you outside?"

She didn't respond. Her entire body seemed to be shivering underneath the blanket. Doc pulled his gloves off and tossed them along with his coat onto the nearby armchair.

"Andie? I need you to sit up for me, love. Can you do that? We need to warm you up." Doc rubbed his fingers together for several seconds to warm them before gently massaging her hands. They were ice cold. "Sit up, love. Come on."

"Doc..."

"You're hypothermic. I've got the fire going. We'll get some tea in you. Where are the spare blankets?" Doc had some training in first aid, having taken a course ages ago. He'd also done a fair amount of research while writing about the Arctic. "Were you trying to escape our conversation this badly?"

"No." Andie stammered the word out. She managed to raise a trembling arm to put toward the hall closet. "Blankets."

"All right." Doc got her sitting up with Rupert pressed against her side. He draped the available blanket around her shoulders. "We'll get you warmed up."

With a bit of digging through the cupboard, Doc

managed to find several quilts. He carried them into the living room. In no time at all, Andie vaguely resembled a mound of shivering fabric.

The kettle whistled in the kitchen. Doc hesitated briefly, tucking in the edge of the blankets. Andie continued to shiver violently.

"I'm going to make tea." Doc didn't even know if Andie had processed anything he'd said since stepping into the cottage. He checked the fire before making his way into the kitchen. "You have herbal tea, right? From your nonna? Anyone with a meditation app addiction has to have herbal tea."

Checking through the cupboards and drawers, Doc eventually found the tea cabinet. He grabbed a large mug and a box of non-caffeinated tea. He also discovered her hot water bottles stashed to one side.

Once the pot of tea was brewing, Doc started the kettle a second time. It took a little while for him to get both bottles filled. Finally, he carried them into the living room along with a mug of tea.

The fireplace had finally begun to warm up the cottage. Andie still continued to shiver uncontrollably. He had to get her temperature up quickly, or they were in for a trip to the hospital.

Sitting on the coffee table in front of her, Doc gently removed her boots and replaced her damp socks with ones he'd briefly warmed up by the fire while making tea. He wrapped the hot water bottle in a spare towel and then placed it under her feet, covering her up again with a blanket.

Doc slipped the second hot water bottle behind her to rest between her back and the sofa. "Think you can manage the mug on your own?"

"Can't...." Andie gave up attempting to take it from him. "Cold."

"Okay." Doc shifted forward and placed the mug in her hands, covering them with his own to provide support. "Can you take a sip?"

"No." Andie's teeth chattered. She didn't seem able to string a complete sentence together. "Need help."

"Right. We'll manage together, love."

It was awkward and slightly messy. But Andie got a few sips of tea. He continued to warm her hands, periodically offering her more from the mug.

After what seemed like ages, Andie stopped trembling quite so violently. She managed to hold the mug on her own. He'd topped it off for her while busying himself in the kitchen.

Scrounging around in the fridge and cupboards, Doc had found ingredients to make a simple chicken, veggie, and rice soup. He'd been halfway through dicing everything up when her tablet made a sound. It was buried underneath a stack of mail that she'd obviously picked up earlier.

"Your nonna's on Zoom." Doc held the tablet away from him like it was contagious. He didn't mind electronic communication, but video seemed unnecessary. "Want me to ask her to call back?"

"I can manage." Andie sounded far better than the hoarse chattering she'd done earlier. "Sorry to be such an absolute bother."

"You're not a bother." Doc answered the call with a short wave before twisting the tablet around and setting it up on her knee. "I'll finish making soup for us."

"What have you done to yourself, Andriana?" Her grandmother switched to rapid-fire Italian. Doc could hear other voices, the rest of Andie's family in the background as well. They were all talking over each other. "Docherty? Where are you? Come back and tell me why she's not saying anything."

"Maybe because you haven't let her have a word in edgewise?" Doc stepped around behind the sofa so they could all see him. He almost laughed at the number of people trying to squash themselves into view on the Zoom screen. "Your Andriana got a little cold. She's going to be fine, but maybe she can call you later when her teeth aren't threatening to break themselves into pieces?"

Alex, Andie's da, waved at him from the bottom corner of the screen. "Take good care of our wee bairn."

"I'm thirty-five," Andie grumbled hoarsely. She shivered and pulled the blankets up higher. "I haven't been a 'wee bairn' in many years."

"I'll take good care of her." Doc waited for all their goodbyes to be said before disconnecting the Zoom call and turning off her tablet. "You okay?"

Andie sank back against the cushion and dragged the unwieldy mass of blankets more tightly around her. "I can't seem to completely warm up."

"Give it time. You'll get there." Doc set her tablet to the side. He offered her the mug of tea for a second time. "How are your hands?"

"A little better." Andie struggled for a few seconds before getting both hands out of the blankets. She clutched the mug in both of them. "Not sure what happened. It was chilly. I couldn't think straight. No idea how I got into the cottage. Rupert kept nudging the back of my legs when I stopped walking. The wind and snow. Everything's a blur. I tried lighting the fire, but my fingers refused to cooperate. Like I'd lost all my fine motor skills."

"Hypothermia can sneak up on you. It's a windy but damp cold out there. Seeps into your bones." Doc returned to the kitchen to check on the soup. "This needs to simmer for another thirty minutes. I'll set a timer."

"Doc? Come keep me warm."

Doc stirred the soup a few times before setting it on top lengthwise to prevent the pot from boiling over. "Just a second."

Settling on the sofa beside her, Doc stretched his arm along the back of it. Andie eyed him briefly before tilting over until she crashed into his side. He chuckled while helping her into a more comfortable position, cuddled against him.

"Feel like a numpty."

"You shouldn't. It can happen to anyone. I bet you were thinking of a quick whiz around the farm to check on everything. You planned to go right back inside. No reason to think you'd wind up hypothermic." Doc adjusted his arm around her shoulders, allowing her to tuck herself closer to him despite the layers of blankets." You warm enough?"

"Nice and toasty. No longer feels like I'm going to rattle my teeth out of my head." Andie sipped her tea in silence for a minute. "Why'd you run away when we first kissed?"

"What?"

Andie tapped her fingers against the mug. "Maybe I'm still rattled by the cold. Just a question that's been floating around in my mind for a while. I shouldn't have blurted it out like that. Sorry."

"Fair question. Just... trying to process my thoughts."

There was another more prolonged silence. Doc thought carefully about the question. It had been one he'd asked himself several times as well.

"Fear," Doc finally responded.

"Of me? Us?"

"Of myself. I didn't understand what I was feeling physically and emotionally. And my lack of interest in sexual shenanigans has been an issue previously. I just... thought something was wrong with me. I didn't want to wreck our friendship." Doc saw the irony in his thinking in retrospect, but he hadn't been ready for the lifelong sort of relationship he hoped they'd have. "I didn't have the words for it then."

"What words?"

"I'm asexual. Those words. I'm asexual." Doc had repeated them to himself a number of times. He'd experienced immense relief at no longer feeling broken but having a way to express who he was.

"Not sure I could've managed a relationship with you until I understood myself better."

"You saying you had to warm up to the idea?" Andie tried to hide her snicker in the blankets.

"Might be the worst joke you've ever told me." Doc stretched his legs out in front of him. He laughed when Rupert made himself comfortable underneath them. "I'm sorry it took me so long to get here."

"Just glad you followed the breadcrumbs back home." Andie offered him her mug of half-finished tea. She gave what seemed like a satisfied sigh and settled back against him. "I knew you'd come back."

"I didn't." Doc placed her mug on the coffee table. "Thought I'd lost my chance. I'm glad I came home."

"Me too."

Chapter 21
Doc

March

MARCH HAD BROUGHT MODERATELY WARMER temperatures. They'd thawed out nicely. Doc had gotten his next round of edits from Essie.

It had taken him days to open the email. He kept pretending not to see the unread message. On the third day, Essie sent him a chicken emoji in a text.

Rude but not wrong.

He managed to open the email without incident. An irrational anxiety, but one he dealt with frequently. There were days when he physically hid his laptop over email stress.

Essie had learned over the years to lightly prod him a few times. Gentle teasing. It usually worked like a charm. She was good at finding the right balance.

And she never expected him to be like her non-autistic authors.

All the windows in the tiny cottage were open. Doc had a perfect view across the farm to where Andie was spending her day planting seedlings. She'd gone into great detail about her plans, but his mind hadn't held onto it.

Some sort of berry.

A strong breeze whistled through the cottage. The wind had picked up a little as the afternoon progressed. He heard Rupert barking in the distance.

Spring hadn't quite fully sprung yet. They had another month or so for that. But hints of it were everywhere around them.

Deleting the next paragraph in the chapter, Doc tapped his fingers against the key while staring out the window. His gaze was unfocused. He saw sentences floating around him while he tried to rearrange them in a way that fit the story better.

"Ah, there you are." Doc sat up from where he'd been slouching in one of the beanbags and began typing away at his laptop. "Progress."

"Talking to yourself?"

Doc was so startled out of his thoughts that he

narrowly avoided dropping his laptop. Instead, he finished typing the sentence before responding to Andie, who'd poked her head through the front window. "The farmer in the pane?"

"Funny. Fancy a tea break? I'm dying for biscuits."

"I'd love to, but I'd lose my train of thought." Doc could already feel his fickle muse dancing on the edge of the cliff. "Just have a few hundred words to add back to this chapter."

"I'll bring you a snack." Andie dashed off without giving him a chance to respond.

Shaking his head, Doc refocused on his manuscript. He wanted to be finished with editing soon. Spring on the farm was a busy time—and he was looking forward to helping Andie.

"Special delivery."

Doc found himself, for the second time in the space of thirty minutes, jolted out of his thoughts. "What's the opposite of a drive-thru window?"

"A walk-up? A walk-in? I'm not sure." Andie had a small tray with a mug and a plate of biscuits. She was balancing it on the window frame, waiting for him to retrieve it. "Thought you could use some fuel to keep you going. I'll be in the orchard if you need me. I've got a long to-do list to make sure all the trees are ready for spring."

An hour later, Doc hit an editing wall. He decided to stretch his legs and wandered out to find Andie. She had a rake in hand and appeared to be inspecting the base of all the trees. Rupert darted over to greet him.

"Are you being a help or a nuisance?" Doc tossed the ball Rupert dropped at his feet. "I'm guessing the latter."

"He's very good at taking away the small branches." Andie paused for a second, then continued dramatically. "And bringing them back to me."

"Why are you sweeping the ground?" Doc stepped over to help her carry a stack of fallen branches to the wheelbarrow. "Victims from the storm?"

"One aspect to my 'defeat pests before they start' plan. Clear out leaves, sticks, and any other mess around the roots." Andie rested her arm against the top of the rake handle. "This will take up much of my day today, thanks to the winter storm. Tomorrow I'll start pruning some of the branches. Meant to do it in February, but it was too bloody cold."

"How can I help?" Doc rolled up the sleeves of his shirt and cardigan.

"What about your edits?" Andie had been going out of her way to avoid distracting him from his deadlines. He'd greatly appreciated her kindness. "Did you get what you wanted done?"

"I've hit a metaphorical wall. If I don't take a break, I might lose the will to finish." Doc bent down to retrieve the ball when Rupert pawed at his leg. He sent it flying down the path between the rows of trees. "So, instead of staring blankly at my manuscript until words lose all meaning, how can I help?"

"We wouldn't want that." Andie tossed another armful of branches into the wheelbarrow. "Storm did a number on the poor trees. Give me a hand clearing up branches and dead leaves? It helps prevent disease and pests."

"Think Mother Nature did the pruning for you." Doc grabbed a second rake resting against the wheelbarrow. He started on the row across from where she'd been working. "Do you ever find the endless cycle of tasks dragging you down? Sometimes with writing and editing, I feel like 'I've done this, so why do I have to do it again?' Essie tells me to have another coffee and quit whingeing."

"Whether we're talking bark or paper, we both have to do the drudgery before enjoying the fruits of our labour. Metaphorical or otherwise. You might say we get to eventually rake in the profits." Andie snickered when he groaned at her attempt at a pun. "Isn't it worth the effort when harvest time comes?"

"So says every farmer, I imagine."

"You're not wrong." Andie pulled off the jacket over her cardigan. "I couldn't do what you do. Sitting in front of a laptop for hours and hours on end? My worst nightmare. I love being outside. Love starting with an empty bed and slowly nurturing little seedlings into a bountiful harvest. It's the closest to magic that I'll ever get."

Doc carried the branches and leaves he'd gathered to drop onto the large pile she'd built. It was packed to the point of being overloaded. He set the rake aside and grabbed the handles of the wheelbarrow. "Where am I taking this?"

"Let me show you. I used some of the timber from the barn we tore down to set up a new place for composting. We'll toss the leaves and some of the small twigs, after I break them down, into the mound. The larger ones can go in the firewood pile." Andie set her rake up against the tree. "C'mon. I'll lead the way."

Wheelbarrows were tricky things. Doc had never been brilliant with them, particularly given his lack of spatial awareness. He struggled to keep it balanced while Rupert dashed around him. It was almost impossible not to get distracted.

"Rups. Stop. You're going to—" Andie lunged forward a second too late when Doc lost his battle with the wobbling wheelbarrow. It tipped over on its side with a spectacular crash. "Well, shite."

Rupert wagged his tail proudly. He snatched one of the longer sticks and tore off down the path. Andie peered over at Doc, whose feet were covered in muck. Her lips twitched a few times before giving into laughter.

Doc tried not to join her but failed miserably. "I swear I haven't been hitting the bottle."

They wheezed with laughter. Doc bent forward briefly with his hands on his knees, trying to control himself. He wiped away the tears from the corner of his eyes while still chuckling.

"Thanks for all the help." Andie managed to get the words out in between bouts of uncontrollable giggles.

Doc offered his arm for support while they both tried to reel in their laughter. "Am I relegated to raking and not driving?"

"Well, I might not hand you the keys to the tractor." Andie collapsed against him. Giggles kept bubbling up out of both of them. "I love you."

"Not for my wheelbarrow skills." Doc looped his arm around her, rubbing her side when she struggled to catch her breath.

"No, for laughing with me instead of getting angry when things go tits up." Andie finally managed to stand up straight. She pressed her hands to her flushed face, still grinning madly at him. "For finding joy in all the silly moments."

"Always found laughter to be a better option over anger or tears whenever possible." Doc hugged her tightly, brushing a kiss to the top of her head. "Well... how about we try this again?"

"Without the drunk driving?"

"Without the mildly chaotic wheelbarrowing." Doc chuckled when she broke into another fit of giggles. "And for the record, I love you as well."

Chapter 22
Andie

April

WHY IS MY FACE WET?

I don't like this dream.

Andie swiped at the wet thing on her face, then groaned when she realised Rupert had gotten on the bed. She pushed his nose away from her ear. "Rups."

Rubbing the sleep from her eyes, Andie gradually eased out from under the blankets and Doc's arm. He continued snoring, utterly unaware of her early morning escape. Rupert followed her down the hall into the bathroom.

"Give me a second." Andie dragged on her thick robe and shoved her feet into her slippers. "Patience, Rups, patience."

Aside from a surprisingly heavy snowfall around the middle of the month, April had brought out what Andie loved about spring the most. Daffodils had bloomed. The fields and trees were beginning to go green again, with sunny skies overhead.

"Why are you always so ready to be awake in the morning?" Andie stared tiredly down at Rupert before starting the coffee machine. She led him outside. Doc had surprised her with a fancy machine to replace her simple electric kettle.

He claimed it was a surprise for her. Andie thought it was more for him. He liked his fancy coffee as much as she enjoyed overpriced kitchen gadgets that she often used once every six months, if that.

It did make good coffee.

Delicious coffee.

"Ready to step outside?" Andie crouched down to give Rupert a good scratch. "You ready?"

Rupert danced around in a circle, knocking her backward. Andie chuckled while he licked her face. She finally managed to get out from under him.

"Shh. You're going to wake Doc up." Andie guided him outside and gently eased the door shut behind her. "Off you go."

Clouds diffused some of the growing morning light. A pinkish-orange hue began to take over from the hazy dark blue of dusk. Andie breathed in deeply; the temperature was just the right side of crisp for her to enjoy.

It was going to be a lovely spring and summer. Andie had hope for the future. All her family had gotten vaccinated, and the world seemed on the precipice of opening up a little at a time.

She hoped to see her parents before another Christmas went by. They had months and months to go since they wanted to wait a while to ensure travel would be safe for her grandparents to come with them. She was holding on to her natural inclination toward cautious optimism.

Wrapping her robe more tightly around her, Andie whistled for Rupert, who'd vanished across the farm. She wasn't quite ready for a trek down the lane. Her fluffy house slippers weren't meant for the outdoors.

The door opened behind her. Doc came up to wrap his arms around her. She leaned back against him.

It was something they did now, hold each other. Andie didn't think she'd ever get used to the change the past year had brought to her life. She sometimes found herself waking up early to watch him while he slept.

Because he was there.

"You're thinking heavy thoughts this morning." Doc rested his chin on her shoulder. His voice was deep and gravelly like always when he'd just woken up. "Do you want to talk about it?"

"Thinking about how I never imagined we could be here when you vanished after we kissed in the orchard."

"I wasn't ready." Doc squeezed her gently. He swayed with her slightly, almost as though they were dancing in the glow from the sunrise. "I had to know myself better."

"In your fifties?"

"You're never too old to learn about yourself, love. Never." Doc was silent for a minute. Andie waited for him, well-versed in his need to carefully put his thoughts together. "I definitely identify as asexual. I watched those videos you shared and read everything you shared with me. It's... freeing to have a word. To have whole paragraphs to express what I've always felt about relationships."

"Powerful, isn't it? Knowing you're not alone."

"Yes." Doc nodded. Andie shivered when his beard tickled her neck. "I can say what I am. Not be ashamed to be who I am. I don't enjoy sex. I've never been sexually attracted to someone. And that's okay."

"It is." Andie had done everything she could to help Doc in discovering his identity. "I'm proud of you. Not easy to teach an old sea dog new tricks."

"I've never once been a sea captain. I just resemble one."

"It's the beard."

"It is." Doc nodded once again. "Not sure I was prepared for a relationship before."

"Then I'm glad we found our second chance when you were ready." Andie whistled for Rupert one more time. He bounded up to them, slipping past them into the cottage. She leaned back against Doc as they watched the sun make itself known over the horizon. "It's a quiet life."

"A nice life."

And it was.

A nice, perfect quiet life on a little farm filled with love and laughter.

"You could say I've gone from farm to Fabre," Andie teased Doc.

"Quite possibly the worst joke you've ever made." Doc stepped back from her with a chuckle. "Coffee's about done. Ready to start the morning?"

Andie nodded, feeling like they were starting more than just their morning. "Just been waiting for you."

"I'm here." Doc smiled when she slipped her hand into his. "Is this an 'I love you' kind of moment? Feels like one."

"I'm glad you're here. And I love you."

"I love you even though you made a terrible farm-to-Fabre joke." Doc laughed when she poked in him the side. "Maybe it should be farm to fable? Because having a happy ending seems more like a fairy tale than anything else."

"A happy ending is a happy ending. You've found yourself a farmer instead of a damsel in distress." Andie led him back into the kitchen. She breathed in the smell of the fire he'd started and the freshly brewed coffee. "And we've got Rups instead of a dragon."

"Good. I have no idea what to do when people are in distress." He leaned against the counter, grabbing the mug he'd made for himself. "If this is a fairytale, then what's the moral of the story?"

"Know thyself before you can kiss under the apple trees?"

Doc snorted into the coffee. "Don't quit your job to become a poet."

"Everyone's a critic. Fine. What's your take on the moral of our story?"

"There is none." Doc took a long sip from his mug. His eyes twinkled when he glanced at her. "Morals come at the conclusion of the story. And ours is barely begun. So why write the end before we've even gotten past the first chapter?"

"Oh." Andie blinked back a surprising burst of emotion. "That's lovely. Maybe that's the moral of the story."

"What?"

"If love is a story, write it a chapter at a time." Andie reached for her mug of coffee. "Instead of trying to skip to the end."

"Good advice."

"And always have your own blanket in bed." Andie laughed when he rolled his eyes. "Duvet thief."

***

We hope you've enjoyed this sweet escapism. Looking for more from Dahlia Donovan, check out ALL LATHERED UP for free. You may also enjoy

THE MISGUIDED CONFESSION, a stunning shifter romance.

Looking for more asexual characters? Check out Dahlia's **MOTTS COLD CASE MYSTERY SERIES** —POISONED PRIMROSE, book one.

Acknowledgments

A massive thank-you to my brilliant betas who take my first draft and help me turn it into something legible. To Becky, Olivia, and all the fantastic people at Hot Tree. And also to my beloved hubby, who keeps me from losing my mind while I'm stressing over word counts.

And, lastly, thank you, readers, for following me on my writing journey. I hope you enjoy this second chance romance as much as I did.

About the Author

Dahlia Donovan wrote her first romance series after a crazy dream about shifters and damsels in distress. She prefers irreverent humour and unconventional characters. An autistic and occasional hermit, her life wouldn't be complete without her husband and her massive collection of books and video games.

Join Dahlia's newsletter:

HTTP://EEPURL.COM/QONOX

Dahlia would love to hear from you directly, too. Please feel free to email her at DAHLIA@DAHLIADONOVAN.COM or check out her website DAHLIADONOVAN.COM for updates.

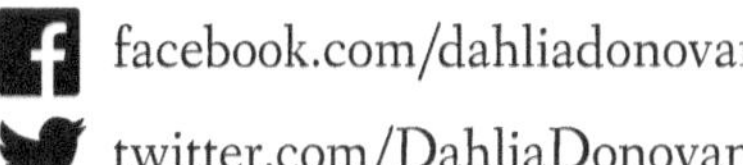

facebook.com/dahliadonovan

twitter.com/DahliaDonovan

instagram.com/dahliadonovanauthor

bookbub.com/authors/dahlia-donovan

About the Publisher

Hot Tree Publishing loves love. Publishing adult romantic fiction, HTPubs are all about diverse reads featuring heroes and heroines to swoon over. Since opening in 2015, HTPubs have published more than 300 titles across the wide and diverse range of romantic genres. If you're chasing a happily ever after in your favourite subgenre, HTPubs have you covered.

Interested in discovering more amazing reads brought to you by Hot Tree Publishing? Head over to the website for information:

WWW.HOTTREEPUBLISHING.COM

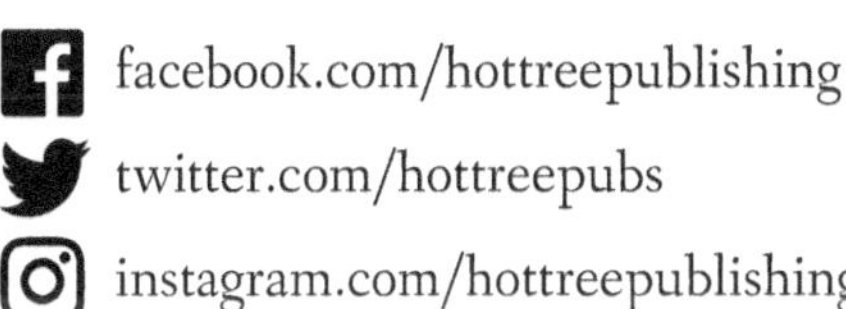

facebook.com/hottreepublishing

twitter.com/hottreepubs

instagram.com/hottreepublishing

9 781922 679444